SHERLOCK JONES

THE MISSING DIAMOND

The Young Refugee Series
Escape to Liechtenstein
The Search for the Silver Eagle
The Incredible Rescues

Sherlock Jones, Junior Detective
Sherlock Jones: The Assassination Plot
Sherlock Jones: The Willoughby Bank Robbery
Sherlock Jones: The Missing Diamond

SHERLOCK JONES

THE MISSING DIAMOND

ED DUNLOP

JOURNEY
FORTH™

Greenville, South Carolina

Library of Congress Cataloging-in-Publication Data

Dunlop, Ed, 1955-

Sherlock Jones : the missing Diamond / by Ed Dunlop.

p. cm.

Summary: Seventh-graders Jasper "Sherlock" Jones and Penny Gordon use their detective skills and faith to identify a software pirate at Diamond Computer Technology, then help solve the kidnapping of the owner's daughter, their new friend Lisa Diamond.

ISBN 1-59166-316-4 (perfect bound pbk. : alk. paper)

[1. Kidnapping—Fiction. 2. Wealth—Fiction. 3. Christian life—Fiction. 4. Mystery and detective stories.] I. Title.

PZ7.D92135Sgd 2004

[Fic]—dc22

2004023220

Design by Craig Oesterling

Cover illustration by Scott Freeman

Composition by Melissa Matos

© 2005 BJU Press

Greenville, SC 29614

Printed in the United States of America

ISBN 1-59166-316-4

15 14 13 12 11 10 9 8 7 6 5 4 3 2 1

Dedicated to all my young friends
at Triple-S Christian Ranch

*"And he said unto them,
Take heed, and beware of covetousness:
for a man's life consisteth not
in the abundance of the things
which he possesseth."*
Luke 12:15

CONTENTS

One   The New Kid   1

Two   Diamond Computer Technology   7

Three   Computer Trap   16

Four   The Catch   23

Five   Cookout   29

Six   The Kidnapping   41

Seven   The Ransom Demand   51

Eight   Disaster!   59

Nine   The Wreck   66

Ten   One Small Clue   74

Eleven   The Pay Phone   80

Twelve   The Rental Agency   84

Thirteen   Desperate Search   90

Fourteen   Volunteers   97

Fifteen   The Butterfly   102

ONE

THE NEW KID

The walkie-talkie on my dresser began to beep softly, and I rolled over in disgust and looked at the clock. It was six thirty. Who on earth would be calling at this hour?

Rubbing the sleep from my eyes, I threw the sheet to the foot of the bed, then stumbled to my feet, and picked up the walkie-talkie. As I switched the unit on, I groggily realized that the caller had to be Sherlock. He had the other unit at his house. I squeezed the black plastic talk bar and held the walkie-talkie up beside my face. "Penny here. Over."

"Penny, how are you?" Sherlock's voice blasted out of the little speaker, and I quickly turned the volume down. "I've been worried about you! Over."

I tried to stifle a persistent yawn and then squeezed the bar again. "All right, I guess. I'm feeling a lot better. Over."

"Are you coming to school today? Over."

"Guess I have to," I sighed. "Mom says my temperature's back to normal. Anyway, I'm glad. It was tough missing the first two days of school. Over." I set the unit on the edge of my dresser and then struggled to pull my nightgown over my head while Sherlock continued to talk.

"Glad you're better," the walkie-talkie told me. "I've been praying for you. Hey, there's a new girl in our class that you'll wanna meet. Over."

I leaned over and squeezed the button. "Who is she?" I was talking right through the fabric of my nightgown, from which I was still struggling to free myself. I forgot to say "over," but Sherlock didn't notice.

"Lisa Diamond," he answered. "You know that giant complex they built east of town, the glass building that reflects all the cars on Highway 69? That's Diamond Computer Technology. Larry Diamond is one of the owners, and Lisa is his daughter. Over."

I was finally free of the nightgown. I glanced in the mirror, wrinkled my nose at what I saw, and picked up the walkie-talkie again. "What's she like? Over."

"Rich. Big time. Diamond Computer had sales of over twelve billion last year, and her dad is the CEO, as well as one of the major stockholders. She comes to school in a limousine. Over."

I snorted as I pushed the talk button. "A real snob, huh? She ought to fit in real well at Spencerville Junior High with all of us poor kids from Willoughby! What do the other kids think of her? Over." I dropped the unit on the bed and selected a clean dress from the closet.

"Hey," Sherlock answered, "she's really nice! She's not the least bit stuck-up. I think you'll like her." There was a funny tone in his voice, something I had never heard before, and I frowned.

I picked the unit up one final time. "Hey, I gotta run. Thanks for checking on me. See you at the bus stop. Over and out."

"Over and out."

I switched the unit off and dropped it back on the bed, then headed for the bathroom. I hadn't even met this new girl, but I already knew that I didn't like her.

After a quick shower, I spent fifteen futile minutes trying to do something with my unruly, unmanageable hair. I gritted my teeth as I pulled the brush through my thin, blond tresses, grimacing in disgust at the freckled face that stared back at me from the mirror. I hated my hair, and I hated those freckles!

Finally I gave up, flopped across the bed, and picked up my Bible. I read through a Psalm—one of the short ones—and headed down for breakfast.

Dad and Mom were already at the table. Dad looked up from his paper. "Hi, sweetheart. How are you feeling?"

I grunted in reply. "OK, I guess." I dropped into a chair.

My pretty Mom stepped over and placed the inside of her wrist against my forehead. "Your fever's gone. Feel up to going to school?"

I nodded. "I'm better. I couldn't stay in bed another day."

Dad gave me a smile. "Why so glum?"

I shrugged. How could I tell him what was bugging me? Sherlock and I have been friends for two years and along comes another girl, and right away he's so impressed with her! I managed a smile. "I'm OK."

Dad folded his paper in half. "It says here that Diamond Computer has hired more than eighty people this past month! That ought to be good for Willoughby's economy."

Mom nodded. "I'm glad they chose our town." I frowned as I poured a bowl of cereal. At least somebody was happy about it.

Mom packed me a lunch, then glanced at the clock as she finished. "It's almost seven thirty. Better catch that bus!"

Five minutes later Sherlock met me at the bus stop, and I stared at him in amazement. He was wearing dress slacks and a sport shirt, and his dark hair was neatly combed. I glanced at his feet and saw that he was even wearing dress shoes! And believe it or not, they were actually shined.

I couldn't believe it. Where were the faded T-shirt, the tennis shoes, and the scuffed blue jeans? Even his unruly cowlick was missing! "You sure look different!" I snorted. "What happened? Did you get a job as a model?"

"We're in junior high now, Penny," he said quietly. "Things are different—a lot different. You'll see."

And then it hit me. It was that girl. Sherlock was dressing up to try to impress her! I gritted my teeth but didn't say anything.

The hiss of air brakes announced the arrival of the school bus, and Sherlock followed me to a seat. I watched in surprise as he carefully placed a stack of textbooks between us. "You haven't memorized your books?"

He shook his head. "Haven't had time yet," he replied, "but I'm working on it. This is only the third day of school, remember?"

I turned to look out the window as the bus roared away from our stop, but Sherlock placed a thin hand on my arm. I turned back toward him. "Wait till you meet her, Penny."

"Meet who?" As if I had any doubt.

"Lisa. You'll like her."

"I guess I will," I shot back. "You sure seem to!" I turned back toward the window. "Rich people and I just don't get along, Sherlock. I can't stand people who are too good for me."

"Lisa's different."

I didn't answer but continued to stare out the window.

"What's she look like?" I asked finally, watching as the bus pulled up in front of a huge, intimidating building. I wasn't sure I was going to like being in junior high.

"Tall, slender, dark hair," my friend answered. "Friendly eyes and a pretty smile."

I grabbed my lunch sack and followed him down the aisle of the bus. As we stepped from the bus, Sherlock stopped and pointed. "Look! Here she comes now!"

I turned and saw a long, black limousine cruise silently up to the front of the school. The driver's door opened, and a uniformed chauffeur stepped quickly around the front of the vehicle and opened the rear door and then stood stiffly at attention.

"Oh, brother."

A slender pair of legs swung out on the sidewalk, followed by a graceful figure in a bright green dress. Dark hair framed one of the loveliest faces I've ever seen in my life. *A pretty smile,* Sherlock had said. That was an understatement. No wonder he was so interested in her!

I turned and saw him standing there quietly. "Well, don't stare," I hissed.

The limousine purred down the driveway, and I watched as it disappeared. "Must be nice," I said. "I'll bet she never has to do dishes, or clean her room, or . . . or wash the car. I'll bet she even has servants do her homework for her!"

"Penny," Sherlock replied in a reproving voice.

Lisa started into the school building and then turned and saw us standing there. To my surprise, she hurried right over. "You must be Penny Gordon!" she bubbled, flashing me a million-dollar smile as she held out a well-manicured hand. "Sherlock has told me all about you!"

I'll bet, I thought to myself. *I can just imagine what he told you!* But I forced a smile as I shook her hand. "I'm Penny," I replied, "and you're . . ."

"Lisa," the girl bubbled. "Lisa Diamond."

"Oh, yeah," I heard myself mutter, "the rich girl."

Lisa sighed. "I get so tired of that," she replied. "Being wealthy isn't all it's cracked up to be."

"I'd trade places with you in an instant," I said and then immediately wished I had kept my mouth closed.

But the other girl didn't seem to take offense. "Don't be too sure," she cautioned. "It has its hassles." She shifted the straps on her book bag. "It's almost time for school to start, and you probably haven't even seen your homeroom. Come on, Sherlock and I will show you around."

Self-consciously I rolled the top of my lunch sack down tighter as I followed this millionaire's daughter through the front door of Spencerville Junior High. At least she is friendly, I grudgingly admitted to myself, for a rich kid. But it's probably just an act. She's new here. Once she chooses her friends, she won't even speak to us.

I decided again that I wasn't going to like her.

TWO

DIAMOND COMPUTER TECHNOLOGY

My first day of junior high went smoothly enough. As it turned out, Sherlock and Lisa were both in my homeroom and had class schedules identical to mine. All I had to do was follow them from one class to another.

Even the teachers weren't as bad as I had expected. They talked tough, and only once during the whole day did I see one of them smile, but they still weren't as fierce as I had imagined them to be. I would live through junior high.

Lunch time brought quite a surprise. I had taken a seat at one of the tables in the huge cafeteria and was just about to sneak a quick prayer over my sack lunch when I saw Lisa hurrying toward me with a loaded tray. "Mind if I sit by you?" she asked and then slid in before I could even reply.

"Why don't you lead us in prayer?" she suggested.

I guess my mouth fell open, and I stammered, "Y-You're a Christian?"

She laughed pleasantly. "Of course. Didn't Sherlock tell you?"

I shook my head. "I didn't ask."

"My dad led me to the Lord when I was seven," she said with a smile. "I was glad when I found out that you and Sherlock are saved too. We'll have some good fellowship. Hey, go ahead and pray for us, would you?"

I stared at her. "Out loud? Right here in front of everybody?"

Lisa shrugged. "Being a Christian isn't anything to be ashamed of you know."

I nodded. "Yeah, right." I bowed my head and led in a short prayer and then went after a tuna fish sandwich.

Lisa took a couple of tablets from her purse and swallowed them with the help of a glass of water. I looked at her quizzically. "Insulin," she explained. "I'm diabetic. I give myself a shot every morning."

I was mildly surprised. I guess it just never occurred to me that rich people could have problems like that too. I felt better already. "Can't your dad get a doctor that can cure you?" I asked.

She laughed. "Money doesn't buy everything, you know," she replied. "There is no cure for diabetes. It can be controlled somewhat by diet or medication, but it's something I'll live with for the rest of my life."

She went on talking cheerfully the whole time we were eating, but I guess I didn't say much. I was busy thinking.

As she picked up her tray I caught sight of a thin, gold bracelet around her wrist. A small gold heart outlined in diamonds hung from the chain. Engraved across the heart were the letters "LAD."

Lisa followed my gaze and realized that I was examining the bracelet. "Isn't it cute?" she asked, holding it up for my inspection. "Daddy got it for me for my twelfth birthday."

"Are the diamonds real?" I questioned.

She shrugged. "I suppose. Daddy wouldn't buy anything else."

"What's 'lad'?" I asked.

She looked puzzled. "Lad? Oh, L-A-D. My initials. Lisa Anne Diamond."

At three o'clock the limousine was waiting at the curb as we walked out the front door. Lisa headed toward it, then turned, and came over toward our bus. "How about coming out to Diamond Computer this afternoon?" she invited. "I can show you around. We don't have any homework yet."

I was dying to see inside that flashy building, but I wasn't about to admit it to her. But as I opened my mouth to decline her invitation, I heard Sherlock saying, "We'd love to come, wouldn't we, Penny?"

I shrugged. "When?"

"I think I know where you live," she answered. "How about if I bike over to your house about three thirty? Sherlock can meet us at your place too."

I stared at her. "You ride a bike?"

Lisa laughed. "Of course. I'm a kid too, you know." She turned and hurried toward the limo. "See you at three thirty."

The bus dropped us off, and I hugged Mom as I hurried up to my room to change. The walkie-talkie began to beep as I was slipping on a pair of culottes, and I snatched it up. "Penny here. Over."

"Well, what did you think of her? Over."

"Sherlock, she was fantastic," I replied, hoping he would catch the sarcasm. "See you in a few minutes. Over and out."

My watch said exactly three twenty as Lisa rolled into the driveway riding an expensive twenty-one speed. I had seen one exactly like it in the Spencerville bike shop for eight hundred dollars. "Nice bike," I commented, hoping I didn't sound too envious.

"Thanks," she said casually, braking to a gentle stop. "Yours is great too."

I looked at her, and by the look on her face, I think she was serious. I was beginning to get the idea that being rich wasn't all that special to her.

Sherlock showed up at exactly three thirty, and we rode leisurely to the glittering Diamond building. As we pulled into the parking lot, I noticed blue glass panels forming a huge diamond over the entrance. The thing must have been thirty feet tall.

Mr. Diamond met us at the door. He was tall, broad-shouldered, and fairly good-looking with short, curly blond hair, and a mustache. But what caught my attention was the way he was dressed—blue jeans, cowboy boots, and a western shirt that was open at the throat. He didn't look anything at all like I thought a millionaire executive should look. He looked more like a cowboy.

But was he friendly! He swung the door open as we approached, gave Lisa a hug as she passed through, and then greeted us warmly. "Come in, come in!" he boomed. "We're glad you're here!" He talked loudly, as though we were still a hundred feet away, but he seemed sincerely glad to see us. I liked him immediately.

A tall, well-dressed woman hurried forward to meet us. She was wearing a very conservative, navy blue business suit with a modest hemline, and high heels that made her legs look like they were going to snap. Her gold jewelry was flashy, but not gaudy. "Well, hello," she said cheerfully, "welcome to Diamond."

Mr. Diamond gestured toward her as though she were an old friend. "This is Irene Lewis, our director of R & D and a vital part of this company."

I leaned toward Sherlock. "R & D?"

"Research and development," he explained in a whisper.

"Irene," the man continued, "meet some friends of Lisa's. This is Penny Gordon, I'm presuming, and this is Sherlock Jones. They're here for a quick tour."

"Pleased to meet you," Irene replied, and it seemed like she really meant it. She turned to her boss. "I could use a break right about now. Mind if I accompany you on the tour?"

"Not at all," Mr. Diamond assured her. "We'll be glad to have your company." He led us down a wide, brightly-lit hallway, and it seemed like we sank two inches into the powder blue carpet. Cheerful paintings graced the walls, and potted plants were everywhere.

"Diamond deals with computer hardware and software," our wealthy guide informed us. "Mainframes are our primary market, of course, but we also have a huge market in PCs and notebooks. We produce educational and business software, as well as top-secret software for military and government applications."

He opened a door, and we saw a large room with two dozen people at work on computers. "They're testing a new software program," he told us. "If there are no major bugs, we'll start marketing next month."

The tour was impressive. We saw labs with programmers writing new programs and rooms with huge machines spitting out software programs on CDs and DVDs. We even saw some PCs being assembled. It was fun.

Finally, on the fourth floor, we came to a locked door, and Mr. Diamond took out a plastic card similar to a credit card. He turned to Irene. "Think I should show them?"

She shrugged. "It couldn't hurt."

He inserted his card in a little slot beside the door. A buzzer sounded, and the door opened by itself. "This is a high-security sector of Research and Development," he informed us. "Normally, you don't get past this door without a security clearance. This is where we develop the programs that are used by NASA, the military, and other government agencies." We looked around for a couple of minutes, but it looked pretty much like the other areas of the building where they were writing programs.

"Daddy," Lisa said, "tell Sherlock about the problem you're having with the pirates." I glanced at Sherlock and could instantly tell that Lisa's comment had caught his attention.

Mr. Diamond looked slightly annoyed that his daughter had mentioned the problem, but he turned to us with an explanation. "Lisa's right," he said. "We have a leak. Someone is pirating a new program that we are developing for the military. We know it's going on, but so far, we've not been able to do anything about it."

"What measures have you taken to stop it?" Sherlock questioned.

Irene stepped forward. "We've put the usual security measures on the research computers, of course," she answered. "Access codes and so forth. We've also divided this R & D sector into four minisectors, each with its own team of R & D personnel. No one works on any part of the project except in his own sector. The access codes are different for each sector. Only Mr. Diamond and I have access to all four sectors. In this way, since it seems to be an inside job, the entire project cannot be jeopardized."

"The entire project is already jeopardized!" Mr. Diamond exploded.

Immediately, he looked embarrassed. "Sorry about the outburst," he told us. "But it's true. We have reason to believe that the pirated information is finding its way to ComTech, one of our major competitors. They have a security clearance to work on military and intelligence programs, just as we do."

A troubled look suddenly crossed his cheerful face. "If ComTech is able to use our research secrets, they could be in a position to underbid us on this project by several hundred thousand dollars. And, poof! There goes a multimillion-dollar contract!"

"What can you do?" Sherlock questioned.

Mr. Diamond smiled. "We have plans. We shouldn't even be discussing this, but you asked, and I don't suppose it can hurt to tell a couple of kids. In about two weeks, we're bringing in a consulting firm to install further security with the capability of tracing the person or persons who are responsible for the pirating. It'll cost us better than a hundred grand."

I whistled in amazement. "A hundred thousand dollars!"

The big man laughed. "At the minimum. That may sound like a lot, little lady, but it will be a bargain if it stops the leak."

We followed the adults back to the lobby. Irene Lewis stepped forward and shook hands with Sherlock and me. "It's been good to have you kids," she said cheerfully. "Stop in any time! If you'll excuse me, I need to get back to work." She gave Lisa a hug and then hurried off to another part of the building.

I watched her go. "She's really nice, isn't she?" I commented.

Mr. Diamond chuckled. "We're fortunate to have her. Diamond Computer wouldn't be the same without her."

Sherlock stepped forward and lowered his voice, speaking to Mr. Diamond. "How long has she been with you?" he asked.

Mr. Diamond didn't lower his voice. "Almost four years," he boomed. "Research and Development has taken off under her expertise."

"Does she hold stock in Diamond?" Sherlock wanted to know.

The executive shook his head. "She's salaried but holds no stock. We give her two hundred grand plus bonuses, and she earns every penny of it!"

The boy detective looked thoughtful. "Miss Lewis mentioned that only you and she have access to all four sectors of the top security R & D," he said. "So how are the leaks occurring in all four sectors?"

Mr. Diamond shrugged. "We're not really sure," he answered slowly. "Irene has been working closely with me on it, and we're doing everything we know to do. We're both at our wits' end. That's why we've finally called in an outside company."

He shook hands with us warmly. "Thanks again for coming. I'm honored to think that my Lisa has you for classmates. As Irene already said, drop by any time."

We thanked Mr. Diamond and headed for the bikes. Sherlock climbed on his bike but didn't go anywhere. He sat quietly thinking for a moment, then exclaimed excitedly, "Yes! I think it will work."

He then pedaled off so quickly that Lisa and I had a hard time catching up with him. As my bike drew abreast of his, he turned to me, his eyes sparkling with excitement behind his thick glasses. "I'm gonna design a program to catch the pirates!" he shouted. "I can do it!"

I'm afraid I laughed in his face. "There's more to it than what you realize, Sherlock. We're talking about some pretty high-tech stuff here."

But Sherlock just pedaled faster. "It's gonna work," he insisted. "Wait and see!"

That evening my parents and I were almost late for the midweek prayer service at church. Pastor Rogers was just stepping to the pulpit to begin the service as we entered, so we hurried to a seat about midway down the aisle. I glanced across the auditorium to see where Sherlock was and got a real surprise. Lisa Diamond was there!

She was sitting with her dad and a plump, pleasant-faced woman that I figured must be her mom. The rest of the pew was crowded full of younger kids.

I watched the Diamond family during the service. They sang the hymns as if they had known them all their lives, and they appeared to be enjoying the service. They seemed to fit right in with everybody else. Watching them, one would have never guessed that they were the wealthiest people in town. I decided that the Diamonds were the most *unusual* rich people I had ever met.

THREE

COMPUTER TRAP

I looked at my watch for the thirteenth time. "Seven thirty-five," I muttered. "Sherlock's gonna miss the bus for sure. I wonder where he is?"

At that moment I heard the growl of the engine as the bus labored up the hill toward me, and my heart sank. Sherlock had never missed the bus during his entire educational career! I heard a shout, and here came Sherlock, sprinting as fast as he could. He reached the bus stop just seconds ahead of the bus and then bent over with hands on his knees, trying to catch his breath.

I stared at him. His hair was uncombed, his socks didn't match, and his shoes were not shined. His shirt clashed horribly with his slacks. So much for the new image. "I thought you were going to miss the bus," I said.

He nodded as we climbed aboard. "So did I," he panted.

I followed him to a seat. "What happened?"

"I overslept," he groaned, as he dropped his bookbag. "I stayed up too late working on the pirate catcher." He gave me a sudden grin. "But it's going to work!"

"Right," I retorted.

He looked at me in surprise. "You don't believe me, do you?"

"Not really," I replied. I sighed. "Sherlock, you're the smartest person I know. Maybe you're even a genius. I've never met anyone else with a photographic memory like yours or anyone that could think things out like you can. But what you are talking about now is impossible! A seventh grader can't just write a computer program to catch a high-tech crook!"

"But I think I can do it, Penny. I know I can!"

"Look," I insisted, "Mr. Diamond is a computer expert, right? And so is Irene what's-her-name. And even they haven't been able to catch the pirates. They're going to spend a hundred grand to bring in outside help to do it for them! Doesn't that tell you anything?"

"I'm going to save them the hundred thousand."

I covered my face with my hands. "Oh, brother. I give up."

By lunchtime I was as hungry as a grizzly bear after hibernation. I hurried through the cafeteria line—Mom had given me lunch money as a special treat—and then found a spot at the table beside Lisa. She looked up as I sat down. "Hi, Penny." She took two insulin tablets from her purse. "Hey, who's your friend? The big guy over there? He was trying to get your attention."

I looked up, and my heart sank. Brandon Marshall. "That's Brandon," I whispered. "He's trouble." On several occasions Brandon and his gang had caused trouble for Sherlock and me, and we usually tried to steer clear of him. I have to admit, though, that he did help us when we had the encounter with the terrorists trying to assassinate the governor.

Brandon carried his tray to our table and sat across from us without even asking. "Hi, Freckles. Hey, who's your good-looking friend?"

"Lisa," I said reluctantly, "this is Brandon Marshall. He was in our homeroom last year. Brandon, this is Lisa Diamond."

Sherlock slid in beside Brandon just then. Brandon unwrapped his sandwich as Lisa said, "Sherlock, why don't you lead us in prayer?"

My gaze jumped to Brandon, expecting him to sneer at us. But to my surprise, he put the sandwich down and bowed his head! Sherlock led in a brief prayer.

When he finished, Lisa looked Brandon square in the eye and asked, "Brandon, do you know the Lord? Have you received Him as Savior?"

I don't know who was more surprised, Brandon or me. But Brandon just shook his head and said, "Nope. But I guess I don't know that much about God."

"He loves you, Brandon," she said softly, "and He wants to save you." She reached in her purse and pulled out a gospel tract. "Here. Read this when you get a chance. It'll tell you more about becoming a Christian."

Brandon reached for the tract, folded it, and stuffed it in his shirt pocket. He took a bite of his sandwich and then mumbled with a full mouth, "Thanks. I'll read it tonight."

I stared at Lisa. She made it seem so easy, so natural, to witness or give out a tract. And then, shame washed over me. I had never even thought to witness to Brandon or offer him a tract, and Lisa does it the first time she meets him!

The next three or four days passed quickly. School was going well, and I was getting in the swing of things. But Sherlock was looking awful! He looked so tired, and he was even thinner than usual.

One afternoon Lisa nudged me in algebra class. "Look at Sherlock," she whispered.

I glanced across and was surprised to see that he was sound asleep.

"Is he getting sick?" she whispered.

"I don't think so," I replied. "But he's working day and night on his 'pirate trap,' and he's not getting any sleep. He will be sick before it's over." I decided to talk with him about it on the way home.

That afternoon I brought up the subject on the bus. "But I'm almost through," he protested. "It's finished, and I'm working the bugs out of it now. I plan to give it to Mr. Diamond tomorrow after school. Will you go with me?"

"I guess so," I halfway promised, "if you'll promise to get some sleep when it's done."

The next afternoon we biked out to Diamond Computer. I followed Sherlock in as he marched right up to the receptionist and asked to see Mr. Diamond. To my relief, we got right in.

"It's good to see you again," the millionaire boomed, shaking our hands and gesturing toward two upholstered chairs. "Be seated. What can I do for you?"

Sherlock closed the door behind us, then took one of the seats, scooting it closer to the desk. "I've been working night and day on a little project for your company," he said. He opened a small paper sack and withdrew a compact disk, laying it on Mr. Diamond's desk. "This is my pirate catcher."

The big man smiled. "I don't understand, Sherlock."

Sherlock leaned closer, and I saw the eagerness in his eyes. "If you'll run this program, it'll trace the pirated programs right to the pirates and list every file they take."

The executive cocked his head. "Where did you get this?"

"I designed it myself," Sherlock said. "I took a basic utilities program, modified it, and combined it with a public domain accounting program."

Mr. Diamond laughed. "That's impossible!"

Sherlock shrugged. "It works. Try it."

But Mr. Diamond just pushed the CD toward Sherlock. "I appreciate it, son, but I'm afraid not. This is a situation for the experts. We're talking high-tech electronics, not basement Mickey Mouse gadgetry."

But Sherlock pushed it right back. "What have you got to lose? Try it. All you need is a laptop with a decent amount of RAM and a modem, plus a free phone line."

Mr. Diamond chuckled. "You're persistent, aren't you? OK, suppose I decide to do it. Tell me how."

A new glimmer appeared in Sherlock's eyes. "Just install the program to the hard drive on the laptop," he instructed. "To run the program, just open it and type 'watch' at the prompt. The computer will do the rest."

He reached back in his paper sack and pulled out a short length of cord with three connectors, two at one end and one at the other. "I noticed the other day that you have eight phone lines. Unplug the phone line from any phone, plug this end into the phone, and then plug the phone line in here. This other connector goes to the USB port on your laptop. No matter which phone line is used, we'll have a record of it."

Mr. Diamond seemed impressed. "You sound like a man who knows what he's talking about."

Sherlock shrugged. "I usually do, sir."

Mr. Diamond stood to his feet. "I won't promise that I'll use it, but I will think about it. Deal?"

Sherlock shook the hand that was offered. "I guess that's fair. Oh, and one more thing. Don't tell anyone about it, OK?"

"No one?"

"Not a soul," Sherlock replied. "It's part of the deal. You should be the only one who knows anything about this. The whole thing has to be kept top secret."

Mr. Diamond nodded. "OK. Thanks for stopping by."

We stopped for a drink in the hallway and then hurried to our bikes. "Do you think he'll use it?" I asked.

Sherlock shrugged. "It's hard to tell. If he does, I'm afraid it'll be just to humor me. He really doesn't believe it will work."

I laughed. "He's not the only one."

We pedaled leisurely along, and Sherlock seemed relaxed for the first time in days. The haunted, tired look was gone from his eyes. I guess Sherlock figured that since the program was in Mr. Diamond's hands now, it was no longer any of his worry.

Halfway home he looked over at me and asked, "What do you think of Lisa?"

"She's all right," I answered grudgingly. "She's friendly enough for a rich girl. And she's always cheerful. I guess I would be too though, if I were as wealthy as she is."

Sherlock shook his head. "Money doesn't make anyone happy, Penny."

I laughed. "I'm not convinced. Lisa's the richest person I've ever known and probably the happiest."

"It's not the money, Penny. Lisa loves the Lord, and He's the source of her happiness. You saw her try to witness to Brandon the other day."

He began to puff as we pedaled up a hill. "If money brought happiness, the Trumps and Kennedys and Rockefellers and people like that would be the happiest people around, right? But you and I both know that's not true. Money can never buy happiness, and it sometimes brings misery and sorrow. That's why God warns us about loving it and about trying to get rich."

I looked at him in surprise. "The Bible warns about trying to get rich?"

"Sure does," he answered "It's in 1 Timothy 6:9. 'But they that will be rich fall into temptation and a snare, and into many foolish and hurtful lusts, which drown men in destruction and perdition.' "

I was quiet for the rest of the trip, thinking hard. If Sherlock was right, then why was Lisa so happy? One thing was for sure, I wouldn't mind being in her shoes for a while!

We reached my driveway, and Sherlock startled me by turning in. "I need to borrow the walkie-talkie back for a while."

I frowned. "But, you said—"

He cut in. "Sorry, Penny, but I need it. Run and get it, would you?"

As I watched him pedal down the drive with the walkie-talkie clipped to his belt, it hit me. He was going to give it to Lisa so he could talk to her! I gritted my teeth. *You little jerk!* I thought. And just when I thought that I could be friends with Lisa.

FOUR

THE CATCH

For the next couple of days, I did my best to avoid both Sherlock and Lisa. I sat with some other girls on the bus, and I ate lunch by myself. If Sherlock wanted to be such good friends with Lisa, that was fine, but he could count me out as a friend. It still hurt to think of him taking the walkie-talkie back just so he could talk to Lisa on it.

But Friday morning he met me at the bus stop as if nothing was wrong between us. I could tell he was excited about something.

"Are you free after school today, Penny?"

I tossed my head. "Probably not."

"I wanted you to come with me to Diamond Computer after school," he told me. "Can you?"

I did my best to act disinterested. "What's so important about going to Diamond again?"

"We caught the computer pirates!" he exclaimed, his eyes gleaming. "I thought you'd want to be there when I tell Mr. Diamond." I was curious, so I agreed to go.

After school Sherlock and Lisa pedaled over to my house, and we all took off for Diamond. As we rode through town, Sherlock said, "We need to stop at Willoughby Drug. I've got some pictures there."

Lisa and I waited outside while Sherlock went in to get his pictures. Lisa was as friendly and talkative as always, but I'm afraid I was a little cool. Sherlock was out in less than three minutes, carrying an envelope of color prints.

He eagerly tore open the envelope, extracted the pictures, and then dropped the empty envelope into his bike basket. His excitement mounted as he thumbed through the pictures. "Yes!" he exclaimed, looking at one photo. He looked at the next and said it again. "Yes!" Whatever he had, he was excited about it. Lisa and I looked at each other and shrugged.

"Look at this one!" Sherlock exclaimed, and we both crowded in close to see the picture.

The photo was of two men and a woman standing beside a car. The woman had a small manila envelope in one hand. Lisa let out a gasp when she saw the picture. "That's Irene Lewis!"

Sherlock nodded. "She's the subject in several others too." He stuffed the photos back into the envelope.

"Sherlock," I asked, "where did these come from? What's this all about?"

"I shot these before school this morning," he replied. "They're for Mr. Diamond." I questioned him further, but he wouldn't say any more.

Ten minutes later, we reached Diamond Computer, and we got right in to see Mr. Diamond. The millionaire greeted us warmly and then offered us seats in his plush office. He turned immediately to Sherlock. "Your program worked, son," he said, "but I'm afraid we didn't catch anything."

Sherlock looked puzzled. "What are you saying, sir?"

Mr. Diamond had the laptop running on his desk, and he turned it around so we could see the screen. "The pirates struck again last night," he replied, "and your program listed fifty-eight files, or partial files, that were stolen by modem. But look at the number it traced them to."

I looked at the screen and saw a whole list of file names. Down near the bottom of the screen were the words "DESTINA-TION: 866-2328."

Mr. Diamond began to laugh. "Do you know whose number that is?" he asked. "That phone number belongs to Irene Lewis!"

Sherlock slid his photos from the envelope and then handed three or four to the executive. "Take a look at these, sir. I shot them this morning behind Smedley's Grocery at 6:28."

Mr. Diamond was puzzled. "That's Irene," he said, rubbing his chin, "but who are the men?"

"This one," Sherlock replied, touching the photo, "is Gary Evans, head of Research and Development at ComTech. The other is David Takamori, who also works—you guessed it—in Research and Development at ComTech."

I watched Mr. Diamond. A look of anger crossed his face, to be replaced moments later by a puzzled frown. "Are you saying that Irene has been pirating our research and channeling it to ComTech? Sherlock, that's absurd! Why would she do such a thing?"

The boy detective dropped a bombshell. "Irene Lewis," he said calmly, "owns thirty-five per cent of ComTech stock."

The millionaire was in shock. As he slowly sat back in his chair, his face was white, and his lips were actually trembling.

"I never would have believed it," he whispered. "How could she do such a thing?"

We sat in silence for several minutes. Lisa walked over and stood beside her father's chair, placing her arm around his shoulder, but I don't think he even noticed. Finally, he looked up, almost as if he had forgotten we were there.

"This was the last thing I wanted to hear," he told Sherlock, "but thank you." He leafed through the photos again. "May I keep these?"

Sherlock nodded. "They're yours. I still have the negatives, of course."

I felt sorry for Mr. Diamond. He looked so discouraged, so tired, and so . . . helpless. The news that his most trusted manager was actually working against him must have been heartbreaking.

He dropped the photos on his desk and looked at Sherlock. "How'd you get these, son?"

"Mrs. Barrett is the town busybody, sir, and she lives right across the street from Miss Lewis. I learned from her that Miss Lewis had been going out early in the morning once or twice a week. She always returned within a very few minutes, so I knew she wasn't going far. My friend Brandon has been watching her house each morning before school for the last two or three days."

Mr. Diamond interrupted. "He was taking an awful risk."

Sherlock shook his head. "Not really, sir, or I would have done it myself. Brandon was in the old fire tower on Signal Hill with a pair of high-powered binoculars. You can see half of Willoughby from up there. He called me on the walkie-talkie this morning when Miss Lewis left the house and then followed her movements with the binoculars and directed me to where she was. He wasn't in any danger whatsoever, sir."

The big man shook his head. "You're incredible!"

He shook hands with both of us again. "I'm afraid we'll be calling an emergency board meeting some time in the next hour. Now, if you'll please excuse me . . ."

We stood to go. "Lisa, stay here with me, please."

I apologized to Sherlock as we pedaled home. "Sorry I didn't believe you," I said. "I never would have thought what you just did was possible."

He shrugged. "No problem. At first, even I wasn't sure." He stood up and pedaled to bring his bike even with mine. "I'll have your walkie-talkie back to you this evening. OK?"

I nodded, too ashamed to tell him what I had thought he had done with it.

It was well after supper when he dropped off the walkie-talkie, probably nearly nine o'clock. "I just got a phone call from Mr. Diamond," he reported. "Irene Lewis denied everything until they showed her my photos. She was fired immediately after the board meeting. Diamond Computer agreed not to prosecute her but only after she made a taped confession of the whole episode. They made her name the other people at ComTech who were involved and list the projects that were stolen and everything. ComTech won't dare use the pirated information to bid against Diamond now!"

I frowned. "But won't she go to jail?"

He shook his head. "That was part of the agreement."

I gritted my teeth. "But look what she did to Mr. Diamond. And he trusted her!"

Sherlock nodded. "She should be incarcerated. But I guess the board at Diamond was trying to minimize their losses and protect their investments. They chose this route."

I was still upset. "I still think she should go to prison!" A sudden thought troubled me. "What if she comes after you? You know, to try to get even?"

Sherlock shook his head. "She doesn't even know who caught her. Mr. Diamond just told her, and the board, that the photos were taken by a detective agency. He didn't say which one."

He turned to go, but I stopped him. "I have just one more question," I said. "How did you know who the men in the pictures were?"

"They both drove cars," he replied, "and cars have license plates. And license plates can be traced. And—"

I cut him off. "OK, OK. I can figure the rest out. Good night, Sherlock."

He pedaled down the drive. "Sherlock!" I called, and he skidded to a stop and looked over his shoulder. "Congratulations!"

He nodded and disappeared into the darkness.

FIVE

COOKOUT

Lisa was waiting as Sherlock and I climbed off the bus Monday morning. "Daddy told me what you and Brandon did for the company," she exclaimed. "I'm not supposed to say anything to anyone you know, because of the danger it might put you and Brandon in, but I just wanted to thank you." With that she hugged Sherlock, and he turned red.

She handed each of us a slip of paper. "You're both invited to a cookout at our place tomorrow night. And your families. But Mom needs to know by this evening, all right? Here's our home number. Have your folks give us a call. See you in a few minutes. I gotta run."

I glanced at the paper after she left and then showed it to Sherlock. "Look at this!" I exclaimed. "She writes her nines backwards!"

He just nodded, as if trying to ignore it, but I persisted. "But why would she do that? She's not in kindergarten."

"Penny."

I turned to face him.

"She has dyslexia, all right? Don't make a big deal out of it."

I wrinkled my nose. "Dis-what?"

"Dyslexia. She sees certain letters and numbers backwards. That's why she has such a hard time reading and why she struggles so hard just to make passing grades."

"Oh." I was embarrassed. "Sherlock, I didn't know. I wasn't making fun of her, honest."

He smiled. "I know."

I was silent as we walked down the noisy hallway toward first-period class, and he noticed. "What's on your mind?"

"I was just thinking about Lisa," I replied. "She has her problems, just like us, doesn't she?"

He shrugged. "Why wouldn't she?"

"Well, you know, she . . ."

"She's rich, right? Penny, wealth doesn't eliminate problems."

I changed the subject. "Think your folks will go to the Diamond's cookout?"

At lunchtime Brandon sat with us, and Lisa gave him an invitation to the cookout too. He shook his head slowly. "Thanks, Lisa, but I don't think so. Mom and I never go anywhere together."

"But ask her," Lisa persisted. "She might come."

"My mom's an alcoholic, OK?" the stocky boy exploded. "She never goes anywhere—unless there's booze." Our area of the cafeteria suddenly grew quiet as other kids stopped talking, and I was suddenly aware of the fact that everyone's attention was on us.

Lisa looked crestfallen. "I'm sorry. I didn't know."

Brandon dropped his head. "Hey, I didn't mean to yell at you, OK? It's just that . . . oh, forget it."

Lisa smiled gently. "It's all right."

I was still thinking about Brandon as Sherlock and I climbed on the bus that afternoon. "Why don't we go out and talk to his mom?" I suggested to Sherlock. "Maybe she'd come if we invited her."

Sherlock thought about it for a moment then shook his head. "I don't know what we'd accomplish," he finally answered. "We might just create a bad scene for Brandon."

"But let's at least try," I urged. "You never know until you try." Sherlock finally relented and agreed to be at my house at three thirty.

He was right on time. We pedaled through town and then took a small road leading north. I had no idea where we were going, but I was confident that Sherlock did. He finally slowed and turned into a narrow, rutted lane, and I followed. Tall oaks grew on each side of the roadway, their branches meeting over-head to form a dark green canopy. The undergrowth on both sides was a tangled mass of brambles and vines, and weeds grew waist high in the center strip of the road. The lane was dark and almost spooky.

"Feels like we're in the African jungle, doesn't it?" I said, almost in a whisper. Sherlock just grunted.

We rode into a clearing and braked to a stop. I gazed at the scene before me and instantly felt sorry for Brandon. The house was hardly more than a shed with a poorly patched roof and a sagging porch. Trash was piled everywhere—old rusting cars, refrigerators, tires, and odds and ends of lumber. Beer cans and whiskey bottles were scattered here and there among the weeds.

A heavy woman sprawled on a dilapidated couch on the porch with an opened beer can beside her. She was wearing the biggest pair of worn-out blue jeans I've ever seen, and her shirt, half-buttoned, looked like it hadn't been washed in two weeks. I haven't been around alcohol much, but I could tell she was drunk. My stomach tightened in fear as we walked toward the porch.

She half-opened her eyes and saw us standing timidly at the edge of the cinderblock steps. "Who are you?" The words came out in a snarl.

Sherlock found his voice. "Mrs. Marshall? I'm Jasper Jones, and this is Penelope Gor—"

"What do you want?" She wasn't even giving Sherlock a chance to answer the original question.

"We came out to invite you and Brandon to a cookout." In surprise, I realized that the second voice was my own. "It's tomorrow evening, at the—"

"Git off my property!" We stood stunned, and she repeated the command. "I said git off! Now!"

The door opened, and Brandon appeared on the porch. Embarrassment was written all over his face. "Ma," he began, "these are a couple friends of mine. This is Penny, and this is Sherlock."

The woman cursed. "I want them gone. Now!"

Brandon gave us an embarrassed, apologetic look. "Ma, they just came out to talk to you."

The beefy woman cursed violently, leaping to her feet in a move that was amazing for someone her size. In a flash, she raised one heavy arm and then swung it sideways at Brandon, striking him in the head. Brandon is a big, muscular kid, but the blow knocked him off balance, causing him to strike his head against the door frame.

To my horror, she was on him in an instant, striking him on the head and shoulders. "Don't never talk back to me, boy!" she screeched. Finally she shoved him sprawling through the open door.

She turned back to us, and I hastily stepped backwards. "Are you leavin' or what?" We didn't need a second invitation.

I was crying as we reached the end of Brandon's driveway. "I didn't know," I sobbed. "I just didn't know!"

Sherlock's face was hard, and his eyes were narrow slits. I've never seen him so angry. "That's alcohol for you!" he stammered, so angry he could hardly get the words out. "Beer and whiskey destroy people!"

His expression suddenly softened as he turned to me. "Brandon needs the Lord, doesn't he?"

That evening Mom called and talked to Mrs. Diamond. I watched as she wrote down the directions to the Diamond house, and I saw her shaking her head as she hung up the phone.

"That's the friendliest woman I've ever talked with," she told Dad. "I was expecting a real snob, but she was really nice!"

I laughed as I entered the kitchen. "It was the same way with Lisa," I said and then told Mom and Dad about the friendship we were developing. I even told them about her witnessing to Brandon. As I mentioned Brandon's name, the episode at Brandon's house popped into my mind again, and I blinked back tears as I told them about it.

"We'll put him and his mother on our prayer list right now," Dad said as I finished. "They both need the Lord."

When I was ready for bed, I called Sherlock on the walkie-talkie, and he answered almost immediately. "Sherlock here. Over."

"Just gonna check and see if your family's going to the Diamonds' for the cookout tomorrow," I said. "Over."

"My parents are as excited about it as I am," Sherlock replied. "I'm anxious to see their place. My dad offered to stop and pick you guys up, and we can all ride together. Mrs. Diamond told us to be there at six thirty. Over."

"I'll accept for my family," I answered. "Plan on us riding with you. It'll be fun. I wish Brandon could go. Over."

"See you tomorrow, Penny." Sherlock sounded sleepy. "Be praying for Brandon and his mom. Over and out."

"Over and out," I answered. "See you tomorrow."

I waited about two minutes and then beeped him again. "Sherlock here. What is it, Penny? Over."

"Good night, Sherlock. Over and out." I switched the unit off and then removed the battery so he couldn't beep me back. I knelt and prayed for Brandon and then was asleep almost as soon as my head hit the pillow.

The next day at school passed slowly. I couldn't wait to go to the Diamonds' house. Each class seemed like it was three hours long.

I saw Brandon once in the hallway between classes. He saw me, hesitated, and then approached shyly. "Sorry about . . ." he fumbled for words, "about . . . about yesterday."

I smiled at him, suddenly wanting so desperately to be a friend to him. I understood now why he always acted so tough, so cool. He was trying to cover up the hurt inside! "It's OK," I whispered, and my voice broke.

He hurried past, but I called softly, "Brandon." He stopped and turned around. "Sherlock and I want to be your friends. We want you to know that." He nodded, swallowed hard and then suddenly turned away.

It was just after six fifteen when the Jones' minivan pulled into our driveway. My dad got up front with Mr. Jones and our two moms sat together in the second seat. Sherlock and I sat in the back. Sherlock is an only child like I am.

Mrs. Jones is kind of quiet, just the opposite of my mom, but my mom more than made up for Mrs. Jones. There wasn't a moment's lag in the conversation. I couldn't really hear how the men were getting along together. Sherlock and I didn't say much.

In just three or four minutes, we pulled into the Diamonds' driveway, and I heard Mom say, "Oh my! I'm going to feel out of place here."

The house was three stories, of dark brown brick, with huge white columns in the front. A circular drive passed in front of the house, and in the very center was a courtyard with a sparkling fountain. The second and third stories each had their own deck extending over one end of the house. A handsome wrought iron fence followed the perimeter of the property, which must have been at least twenty acres. The whole place reminded you of a ritzy hotel or country club.

Lisa came bouncing out to the car to meet us, followed by several younger kids. "I'm glad you could come," she said brightly, opening the door of the minivan for Mom.

"These are my brothers and sisters," Lisa said. "There are six of us kids, you know." Sherlock and I turned and looked at each other, and it was hard to tell who was more surprised.

Mr. and Mrs. Diamond were waiting for us on the porch, and we stepped up and greeted them. It must have taken a full two minutes to make all the introductions.

"We're glad to have you all," Mrs. Diamond said sweetly. "Come on in." She led the ladies into the kitchen.

Mr. Diamond turned to the men. "I'm grilling steaks out on the back deck," he said. "Care to come supervise?"

I stepped inside the foyer and stood speechless. A huge chandelier hung directly overhead, its many lights reflecting like diamonds on the highly polished marble floor. A spectacular circular staircase directly in front of us led upstairs, and skylights overhead bathed the room with a soft multicolored light. This place was a mansion!

We followed the men to the deck, and the little kids all followed us. I stepped over to the biggest barbecue grill I've ever seen to check out the steaks, and Sherlock sauntered to the railing and peered over at the yard below. "Penny! Check this out!"

I leaned over the rail and stared in amazement. Directly below us was a huge swimming pool, shaped just like a guitar! A huge, shimmering blue guitar! A concrete island in the center was placed exactly where the hole would be in a real guitar. I leaned far over the railing and, to my astonishment, saw that the neck of the guitar was a narrow channel running right into the house. "Sherlock! Look at that."

Lisa followed us over, chuckling at our fascination with the pool. "Mom and Dad can enter the pool from their bedroom and swim right out into the backyard."

"Couldn't a burglar enter the house the same way?" Sherlock asked.

Lisa shook her head. "Not really. I'll show you why on that part of the tour. Come on, I'll show you the house." We entered the house with all of her brothers and sisters tagging along, but Lisa didn't seem to mind.

The place was elaborate. But the things that impressed me most were the light switches. When we walked into Lisa's bedroom, the lights came on automatically! I stopped in astonishment. "What in the world—"

"Body heat activated?" Sherlock guessed, and Lisa nodded.

"How do you sleep at night?" I asked.

"You can always turn them off manually," Lisa answered, "but they're also timed. Mine is set to turn off at 9:32, two minutes after my bedtime. Hey, watch this."

She walked over toward a humongous mirror. When she touched a switch, the mirror slowly slid back, revealing an enormous closet! I stepped inside, and as I expected, saw enough clothes to fill a department store.

I stepped back out just as Lisa raised her voice and said, "Kitchen! When's supper, Mom?"

The answer came from an invisible speaker somewhere over our heads. "It'll be at least twenty more minutes, Lisa."

That one caught Sherlock's attention. "Neat," he exclaimed, craning his head back to examine the ceiling. "A voice activated intercom system."

We toured the entire house, and I saw electronic stuff that I didn't even know existed: toilets that flushed by themselves, a shower that delivered water at exactly the temperature you selected by digital thermostat, and wireless stereo speakers in every room. It was like something out of science fiction, the house of the future, or something.

When we reached the master bedroom, we saw the other end of the pool. It had a little white wrought iron railing around it—to keep you from stumbling into it by accident, I guess. "Awesome," I said. "Can you imagine having a pool in your bedroom?"

Lisa pressed a button on the wall, and a thick Plexiglas panel slowly dropped into the pool, blocking the access from the outside. She turned to Sherlock. "Does that answer your question?"

We completed the tour and then hurried to the deck for dinner. Mr. Diamond asked six-year-old Tommy to pray, and he did so without hesitation.

The steaks were huge, and were they delicious! Mrs. Diamond served potato salad, fruit salad, and croissants with the meal and strawberry shortcake for dessert. I noticed that she was as friendly as her husband and daughter.

As we finished our meal on the deck, the millionaire turned to Mr. Jones. "Your son saved my company from disaster," he boomed. "I guess this little party is our way of celebrating and also saying thank you. But we'd like to do more than that." He pulled a check from his pocket. "This check is just a fraction of the amount he saved us."

Mr. Jones glanced at the check, and his face registered his surprise. "Ten thousand dollars! Larry, we can't take this."

The millionaire smiled. "I don't see why not. The boy saved me at least ten times that amount."

I was stunned. Ten thousand dollars! Sherlock was rich.

But Mr. Jones was still shaking his head. "That much money would ruin the boy, Larry. He wouldn't know what to do with it."

"Put it away for college then," Mr. Diamond insisted. "He earned the money."

But Mr. Jones continued to refuse the money. "Let it keep for a few days," he said finally, "while I think on it a while."

"Fair enough," Mr. Diamond agreed, tucking the check back away. "But don't wait too long, or I'll have to add interest to it."

Sometime later we headed for the minivan. I called Mr. Diamond to one side and told him, "If Sherlock's dad won't let him take the money, I know something he would like."

The big man leaned closer. "Name it, little lady."

"A Queen Alexandra's Birdwing," I answered.

He frowned. "What in the world is that?"

"It's a giant butterfly. I don't know where in the world you'd find one, but I know it would be special to Sherlock." I told him how Sherlock had given his own specimen away when we were trying to solve the Willoughby bank robbery.

"What's it called again?" When I told him, he pulled an index card from his pocket and wrote it down. "He'll have it!"

On the way home, I turned to Sherlock. "Ten thousand dollars! Sherlock, he wants to give you ten thousand dollars."

The vehicle was dark, but I could still see the smile on his face. "Ten thousand dollars," he repeated. "And you think that will make me happy, right?"

I sighed. "If it doesn't, just give it to me, OK?"

"Penny, Penny. All you think about is money."

"That's not true," I retorted. "But I do think about it some. After all, it's part of my name."

After I went to sleep that night, I dreamed that someone offered me ten thousand dollars. I accepted immediately.

During the next two days, I hardly heard a word during class. My mind was still on the ten thousand. When I asked Sherlock about it at lunch on Thursday, he just shrugged. "I guess it's up to my dad," he said casually.

I stared at him. "You're not excited about it at all, are you?"

"Some," he admitted. "But I'm not gonna get all worked up about it. Dad may say no."

That evening as Mom and Dad and I were finishing supper, the walkie-talkie began to beep, and I rushed upstairs. "Penny here," I answered. "Let me guess. Your dad is gonna let you accept the money! Over."

"Forget the money," came Sherlock's somber voice.

I wasn't prepared for what he said next. "Penny, I've got some really bad news. Lisa was kidnapped today! Right after school."

SIX

THE KIDNAPPING

I stared at the walkie-talkie, unable to believe what I had just heard. "No!" I cried, "it can't be! Not Lisa!" I squeezed the talk button. "Sherlock, what happened?"

"Don't say a word to anyone except your mom and dad," Sherlock warned, "and make sure they understand the need to keep it quiet. It happened as the chauffeur was driving Lisa home from school.

"The limousine was forced to a stop by two city garbage trucks at the railroad overpass. A man opened the driver's door and maced James Underwood, the chauffeur, and then dragged Lisa from the car. The chauffeur never saw the men or the getaway vehicle. Over."

"And the garbage trucks were hot-wired, right? Over."

"You guessed it. Probably no lead there. Over."

"How did you find out about it," I asked, "since it's so hush-hush? Over."

"I'm not at liberty to even tell you that right now, OK? Pray for Lisa and for the Diamonds. Gotta run, Penny. Over."

"Sherlock," I begged, "please tell me this is just a joke. Over."

I heard him sigh. "I wish I could, Penny, I wish I could. Over and out."

I stumbled downstairs in a daze. Dad saw the look on my face and rushed to my side. "Penny! What's wrong?"

I burst into tears. "Oh, Dad," I wailed, "they took Lisa! They took Lisa!" Dad led me to the couch and gently helped me to a seat. He sat close, and I buried my head against his shoulder. "Dad, they took Lisa!" I sobbed again.

I guess Mom hurried into the room just then because I suddenly heard her voice. "Penny, what's wrong? What happened?"

"Something about Lisa," Dad answered. "I'm still not sure what she's saying."

"It's Lisa," I sobbed again. "She was kidnapped!"

"Oh, no," Mom gasped. "When did it happen?"

I took a deep breath and lifted my head to face them. "Just after school," I replied. "The chauffeur was driving her home from school, and some trucks forced them to stop at the railroad bridge. They took Lisa, and the chauffeur couldn't even stop them 'cause they had sprayed him with mace! Oh, Dad, what are we going to do?"

"The very first thing we need to do is pray," Dad replied, and we all got down by the couch and asked God to watch over Lisa and bring her back safely. When we finished, I felt better. What do unsaved people do when trouble comes, since they don't have a heavenly Father?

"Have the kidnappers contacted the Diamonds?" Dad asked. "Have they made any ransom demands?"

I wiped my eyes. "I don't know. Sherlock didn't tell me much, and he said not to tell anyone but you and Mom."

Mom spoke up. "I can understand that," she said. "If the news gets out, it could create real problems for the family and for the police."

"Have they contacted the police?" Dad asked.

I shook my head. "I don't even know. Dad, let's call the Diamonds and tell them we'll do anything to help!"

Dad shook his head. "Not tonight, sweetheart. Our call would just add more confusion to the situation. But we can pray."

I went out into the backyard and climbed up into the apple tree that hangs over the storage shed. I hadn't climbed it since I was little, but I just wanted to be alone for a while. "God," I prayed, trying not to cry again, "You know where Lisa is. Be with her tonight, and help her not to be afraid. I'd be terrified if it happened to me, Lord, and I just know she's afraid too.

"And be with her mom and dad, and all her brothers and sisters. I'm sure they're hurting too. And, Lord, speak to the kidnappers. Help them to see that what they've done is wrong, and don't let them hurt Lisa." I couldn't help myself; I was sobbing again. "Lord, forgive me for being so cool to Lisa when she was just trying to be my friend."

I stayed up in the tree until Mom came outside. "Penny?"

"Yes, Mom?"

"Where are you?"

"Up here, Mom."

She peered up into the darkness and finally spotted me. "Penny! Whatever are you doing up there?"

"Just praying." I slid down to stand beside her.

"God hears you just as well when you're on the ground as He does when you're up in a tree, you know."

I laughed in spite of my tears, and Mom put an arm around me. "Oh, honey, I feel so bad for the Diamonds." As we walked back to the door I could see that there were tears in her eyes too.

She reached for the doorknob, and I reached out and caught her hand. "I can't go to school tomorrow, Mom. I can't! I won't even be able to look at the other kids without crying, and they'll know something's wrong, and we're not supposed to tell, and—"

"I suppose you're right. I'll talk to Dad. You can skip, just this once."

I tossed and turned all night. I had finally drifted off when the walkie-talkie began to beep. The clock said seven thirty.

"Penny?" Sherlock didn't even wait for me to acknowledge his call. "I'm heading out to the Diamonds' house, and I thought you might want to come. Over."

I was out of bed in an instant. "I'll be ready in ten minutes. Can you stop by here? Over."

"See you in ten minutes," Sherlock replied. "Over and out."

I washed my face, threw on some clothes, and dashed downstairs to find something to eat. Dad had already left for work, and Mom was getting breakfast ready. "Can't stop for breakfast, Mom," I said, throwing a pastry in the toaster. "Sherlock's coming by in less than ten minutes. We're going out to the Diamonds' house."

"Honey, I think you should wait—" Mom began, and then paused uncertainly. "Oh, go ahead," she decided. "Maybe you can be an encouragement to them. Tell them we're praying."

"Thanks, Mom!" The pastry popped up shortly, and I grabbed it and was out the door. I sat on my bike for five minutes waiting for Sherlock.

We rode quickly to Lisa's house. "I almost went last night," Sherlock told me, "but I wasn't sure what I could do. I stayed awake most of the night praying."

"So did I," I replied. "Sherlock, what's going to happen?"

We reached the Diamond estate, parked our bikes in front of the five-car garage, and then hurried to the front door. To our dismay, Officer Clark was at the door. "Sorry, kids," he said, "but I can't let you in. Run along now." He almost seemed sorry, which was unusual for him.

"It's important, sir," Sherlock said, but Clark shook his head.

"Sorry, Sherlock, can't do it."

I turned to go, but at that moment, Mr. Diamond opened the massive front door. "Penny! Sherlock! Come on in!" He turned to Officer Clark. "It's OK." The lawman just nodded.

As I entered the house, I glanced up into Mr. Diamond's face. His eyes were red and puffy, but he made eye contact with me and smiled briefly. I could imagine how he must be hurting, and my heart went out to him. "I'm sorry, Mr. Diamond, I—" my voice broke, and my eyes misted up.

He hugged me. "Thank you, Penny."

Mrs. Diamond hurried into the foyer, followed by Officer Bill. When she saw me, she grabbed me in a hug. I didn't say anything. I couldn't.

"The kids and I are going to my mother's for a few days," she told me, "since the FBI men are using our house for a command center and staying in the guest rooms downstairs. Pray for us."

I nodded.

Officer Bill stepped over and patted my shoulder and then shook hands with Sherlock. "Chief Ramsey has been out of town, but he should be arriving shortly. The FBI sent two agents last night, and several others are checking the crime scene right now. We're doing everything we can."

Sherlock glanced at Mr. Diamond and then turned back to Officer Bill. "Has there been a ransom demand?"

The officer shook his head. "I can't discuss it, Sherlock."

Sherlock turned back to the millionaire. "We're here to help in any way we can, Mr. Diamond. Perhaps we can do leg work for some of the agents, or—"

Mr. Diamond cut him off. "Thanks, Sherlock," he said gently, "but I'm afraid this is police work. As much as we want to get involved, we'd better let them do it, all right?"

Sherlock shrugged and didn't say anything, but I could tell he was keenly disappointed.

"Pray for Lisa, though, will you?" the big man asked. "And for us." We both nodded.

I hugged Mrs. Diamond again. We both shook hands with Mr. Diamond and then stepped outside. Sherlock was very disappointed, and I felt like crying. Officer Clark gave us a sympathetic look.

Chief Ramsey was just pulling in as we pedaled out of the driveway. We waved at him, but he rolled down the window of the police cruiser and motioned for us to come back. He waited for us while we turned around and rode back into the driveway.

"Where are you heading?" he asked Sherlock.

My friend shrugged. "Home, I guess. We wanted to help, but they turned us down. Said it was police business."

The chief pointed sternly to the house. "Get back in that house. That's an order!" He pointed at me. "You too, Missy!" Then he grinned.

Sherlock returned a grin of his own as he saluted. "Yes sir, Chief!"

We followed the lawman back to the door, which Clark opened for us without a word. Officer Bill ushered us into the spacious living room and introduced the chief to the two FBI agents.

Both men shook hands with Chief Ramsey, and the shorter one, Agent Meadows, said, "Chief, good to meet you. I'm in charge of the task force, and I want you to know that my men and I will do everything in our power to assist your department in the safe return of the girl and the apprehension of the kidnappers. Let us brief you quickly on the entire situation, and then we can get down to work."

It was then that he noticed Sherlock and me. He turned to Officer Bill. "The kids will have to go."

Chief Ramsey held up one hand. "Wait. I asked for them to be here."

Agent Meadows snorted. "What?"

The chief stood firm. "I want them here. I'll take full responsibility for both of them. The boy has more gray matter than both you and me put together, and this is one case where we're gonna need it. They stay."

Meadows eyed the chief uneasily. "You don't know what you're asking, man."

Chief Ramsey stood his ground. "They're my responsibility. They're working for my department, not for the Bureau. I need them here! Lisa Diamond's life is going to take precedence over anything else."

Agent Meadows shook his head. "Have it your way. Now we'd better get down to work."

The two men sat down at the kitchen table, and Sherlock pulled up a chair and sat beside Chief. I stood quietly to one side, trying to stay out of the way.

"Here's what we have," the FBI man said. "At approximately 3:10 yesterday afternoon, James Underwood, the chauffeur, was approaching the railroad overpass on Naples Road, driving the Diamond limousine with Lisa Diamond in the rear seat as a passenger.

"As Underwood slowed due to the narrow confines of the overpass, a Spencerville city garbage truck suddenly backed across the north end, and he braked hard to avoid a collision. Another city truck swung in behind him, boxing in the limousine. Underwood reports that his door was suddenly wrenched open, and the next thing he knew, he was being sprayed with mace at close range, rendering him helpless. He was vaguely aware of a struggle in the rear seat, but he did not realize that Lisa was being abducted.

"Approximately ninety seconds later, another motorist was attempting to help him from the car. That's all he can tell us.

"Your officers were on the scene within twenty minutes, and we were called at 5:28. We placed agents on the scene before 7:30. Three footprints in the dust at the roadside indicate that the kidnappers walked back under the overpass with their victim, apparently to a waiting getaway car."

Sherlock interrupted. "Any eyewitnesses?"

The agent turned to him. "Apparently none. At least none have come forward. The motorist who assisted Underwood is an electrician by the name of Rick Dotson, but apparently he drove up just after the kidnappers left the scene."

"Have you canvassed the area for witnesses?" Chief Ramsey asked. "Made an appeal on local television?"

"Teams are out right now," Meadows replied. "But they're forced to be very discreet. The nature of the crime precludes a media appeal at the moment."

"The city trucks were hot-wired?" Sherlock asked.

"Yes."

"And no fingerprints."

"Correct."

"Did the second truck approach from behind or from the side?" the boy detective asked.

"From the side," the man answered. "Sibley Street intersects with Naples less than thirty feet from the overpass."

Sherlock nodded. "I'm familiar with the location. The truck approached from Underwood's left, I assume?"

Meadows looked shocked. "Now how would you know that?"

Sherlock shrugged. "Several reasons. If the truck approached from the left, the driver would be less visible to the limousine as it approached the overpass. Secondly, the driver's door would be closer to the limousine when it stopped, meaning he could reach it quicker. And lastly, the truck would shield him from the view of any motorists coming up behind the limousine."

The agent stared at the boy detective. "You're incredible!"

Sherlock leaned forward. "And the driver of the second truck was the one who maced Underwood."

Meadows shook his head. "We're not sure. Underwood didn't see his attacker."

Sherlock smiled. "That's how I know it was the driver of the truck behind the limousine."

The agent frowned. "How do you figure?"

"Simple," my friend replied. "If it had been the driver of the first truck, the one in front of the limo, Underwood would have seen him approaching!"

Meadows shook his head. "You're making me look bad, kid." He turned to Chief Ramsey. "I'm beginning to see why you wanted this genius along."

Chief grinned and gave me the thumbs up sign behind the agent's back.

SEVEN

THE RANSOM DEMAND

I took a deep breath, let it out slowly, then sank into a chair at the end of the table, as far from the FBI agent as I could get. I was still trying to stay out of the way as much as possible. It was hard to believe this was really happening, and especially, that it was happening to my friend Lisa. I prayed for her again silently, wondering where she was and what she was feeling.

"Tell me about the phone call," Chief Ramsey was saying.

Agent Meadows drummed his fingers on the tabletop. "As you may already know, the call came here," he replied, "yesterday, somewhere around four thirty. A male voice informed Mrs. Diamond that her daughter had been taken from the limo, that she was fine and was being well taken care of. The caller promised further contacts regarding payment of ransom and then abruptly hung up."

"No amount was mentioned?"

"Not yet."

"And that was the only contact."

"The only one so far."

"Did caller ID give an origination number for the phone call?" The question came from Chief Ramsey."

"Nothing. The number was blocked."

Sherlock leaned forward. "You've put trace equipment on the phones, I assume?"

The agent nodded. "Here at the house and at Diamond Computer."

"Including recorders?"

"Yes. Any further calls will be recorded, and if possible, traced to the source."

Chief Ramsey leaned back in his chair with an aggravated look on his face. "Then about all we can do is wait."

Sherlock spoke up. "And pray."

We didn't have long to wait. At that moment, another agent stepped into the room. "Chief," he said, addressing Agent Meadows, "the call just came in. We thought you'd want to hear it."

Meadows rushed from the room on the heels of the other agent, and we started to follow; but Chief Ramsey held up one hand and shook his head, then went after them. Sherlock and I waited for what seemed like an eternity wishing we could hear what was going on.

Finally the men came back into the kitchen. Meadows was carrying a cassette tape, which he popped into a tiny recorder that he pulled from a briefcase. Sherlock and I leaned forward eagerly.

An agent entered the room just then. "The phone booth on Main Street, right here in Willoughby," he said to Meadows. "Larson and Perry are dusting the phone for prints right now, but we don't expect any leads."

The FBI man nodded, and the other agent left the room.

Meadows started to switch the tape recorder on, then paused and looked at Sherlock and me. "Nothing leaves this room, hear? Anything you hear on this tape is strictly confidential."

"You don't have to worry about these two, Meadows," the chief said, and I felt really good inside. Quite a change from the first time we met Chief Ramsey!

Meadows shrugged and switched the little machine on, and then we heard the tape of the phone call. "Hello?" It was Mr. Diamond's voice.

"Diamond?" This time it was a stranger's voice, a tough-sounding man.

"This is Larry Diamond." I was amazed at the calmness of his voice, though I could detect a trace of nervousness.

"Diamond, listen carefully. Don't bother to trace this call; I'll only be here thirty seconds. We have the girl. Here, listen."

We heard the click of a button, and then Lisa's voice. "Daddy? I'm OK." She began to sob and then, "I'm afraid, Daddy. I'm—"

Her voice cut off suddenly, and we heard the man's voice again. "That's enough. Listen carefully, Diamond. We want two-point-four million dollars in cash—two million in hundreds, four hundred thousand in tens and twenties. Start getting the money, and we'll contact you later today. You have eight hours." There was a click and then a dial tone.

Meadows shut the recorder off. "Well, there it is. Diamond is calling right now, making arrangements for the money. That's a lot of cash on such short notice."

"Make up some dummy packages," Chief Ramsey suggested, but the FBI man shook his head. "Diamond's against that. He won't even consider it."

At Sherlock's request, the tape was played again twice. "Well?" Chief said, looking hopefully at Sherlock. "Any clues?"

But the boy detective slowly shook his head. "Not that I can pick up on."

He stood up and addressed the chief. "Penny and I will be home in an hour. Call us as soon as you hear from the kidnappers again, will you?" Chief Ramsey nodded.

I looked at Sherlock in surprise but followed him from the room without protest. "Why don't we stay here?" I asked as we reached our bikes.

But Sherlock shook his head. "They'll call us when something happens. I know Chief Ramsey. But right now, we've got other work to do."

We pedaled downtown and parked our bikes in front of Smedley's Grocery. "What are we doing here?" I asked.

"This is the phone the kidnappers used," he replied, stepping into the phone booth at the corner of the store. I followed him in, noticing that the booth was nearly hidden from the street by a dumpster. Sherlock took a handkerchief from his pocket and lifted the receiver, then studied it closely. "They already dusted it for fingerprints," he said.

We stayed in the booth for another two or three minutes while Sherlock examined it for clues. A look of keen disappointment was on his face as we finally exited. "Nothing," was all he said.

We biked over to the railroad overpass on Naples Street. Sherlock pulled over to the side and braked to a stop about fifty yards from the overpass, so I did the same. We sat silently for about a minute, just staring at the bridge. Finally I asked, "What are we doing?"

"I'm just visualizing what happened yesterday, so I know what to look for," he replied, never taking his eyes off the overpass. I sat quietly so I wouldn't disturb him again.

We walked our bikes closer, finally leaving them on the gravel shoulder of the road. Sherlock glanced back to ascertain that no cars were coming, then walked out almost to the centerline, turned, and walked slowly through the overpass. He did it three times. Next he stood in the roadway beside the stop sign on Sibley Street, staring intently down Naples. Finally he walked through the overpass and examined the roadway on the north side of the bridge.

"Whatcha looking for?" I asked, but he just waved his hand in a motion that seemed to say, "Don't bother me." So I decided to be quiet and just watch.

"There's where the first truck was parked," he remarked, pointing to an almost invisible lane that led into the woods beside the road, "and unless I miss my guess, the getaway car as well. They chose a perfect location for the crime!"

We walked a short way down the lane, Sherlock pausing here and there to examine something more closely. He pointed out the spot where a heavy truck had been parked, and then a short distance further, a car. He whipped out a tape measure and measured the area where the car had been, writing the figures on the back of his hand in green ink.

As he put the pen away, I ventured to ask, "Well, what did you learn?"

He turned and looked at me with a very serious expression. "There were two kidnappers," he said. "One was about six-four, dark hair, mustache. Works as a machinist, used to be in the navy, and has an anchor tattooed on his chest.

"The other man was shorter, about five-ten, with blond hair, balding in the middle. At one time or other he worked for Pepsi-Cola, and he's diabetic.

"The getaway car is a silver 1996 Taurus with a red interior and Wisconsin plates. They just had it tuned, but the tape deck isn't working properly. That's all I can tell."

I had seen Sherlock in action before, but this was amazing. "Wow!" I exclaimed, looking at the lane, "you can tell all that? Sherlock, that's incredible!"

He shook his head. "I wish." He grinned suddenly. "I just made all that up, but it sounded pretty good, don't you think?"

"You little—" I swatted at him, and he ducked away, laughing.

We walked back to the bikes, and suddenly he was dead serious. "The area is clean as a whistle, Penny. The kidnappers, whoever they are, are being very careful. They didn't leave a single clue, in the phone booth, here, or during the phone call. But if they slip up, just once, we'll be ready."

We climbed on the bikes. "I did learn two things here though," he said brightly.

I looked at him, ready for another joke, but he was serious. "What's that?"

"There are only two kidnappers, and they're using walkie-talkies."

"Oh, come on, Sherlock." There was absolutely no way he could know that, so I decided he was teasing me again.

"No, I'm serious," he insisted.

"How can you tell?"

"You saw where the getaway car was parked," he replied. "If there had been three kidnappers, they never would have left it there."

"Why not?"

"The car was parked there for several hours, greatly increasing their chances of it being spotted."

"It was a little ways into the woods," I argued.

"True," he replied. "But there was the chance of someone stumbling across it. They also ran the risk of someone noticing them as they dropped it off, or of someone seeing the other car."

"The other car?"

"They didn't walk all the way to Spencerville to steal the garbage trucks."

"So they dropped off the getaway car and then drove another car to get the trucks, leaving it somewhere in Spencerville."

Sherlock nodded. "Penny, these men are being very cautious. They're not leaving a single clue. They haven't messed up even once. That's why I say that they would not have left that car unless they absolutely had to, which means just two kidnappers."

"What about the walkie-talkies?"

"You saw for yourself where the truck was parked. There was no way the driver would know when the limousine was approaching, unless the other kidnapper signaled him. The easiest way would be a walkie-talkie."

"Maybe he stood by the roadside and watched for the limo," I suggested, "and then ran to the truck."

Sherlock shook his head. "The timing had to be perfect," he argued. "If the truck backed out too soon, Underwood could have avoided it by turning either way onto Sibley. If the truck backed out too late, the limousine would already have passed."

He glanced at his watch. "Let's head for home," he said. "I'll call the Diamonds' house and tell Chief what we've learned, and then I need to get working on a project. Lisa could lose her life unless we can stop the kidnappers!"

A sudden thought struck me with the swiftness and shock of a lightning bolt, and I turned to Sherlock excitedly. "I know the name of one of the kidnappers!"

I saw a startled look pass over his face. "You do? Who, Penny?"

"Irene Lewis!" I declared in triumph. "Who else? She knew the Diamonds' schedule intimately, and she certainly would have a motive for kidnapping Lisa."

He nodded thoughtfully. "It's a possibility. We can't afford to assume until we have some evidence, but it's certainly a possibility." His back tire shot gravel as he took off suddenly, and I pedaled furiously to catch up.

EIGHT

DISASTER!

I spent a couple of hours up in the apple tree again, thinking, praying for Lisa, and mostly just worrying. What if Mr. Diamond couldn't get the cash together in time? What if he did get the money but the kidnappers didn't release Lisa? What if they killed her? I hated the suspense.

Finally, when I couldn't stand it any longer, I went to my room and called Sherlock on the walkie-talkie.

"Sherlock here," he answered. "Over."

"Sherlock, have you heard anything? The suspense is killing me! Over."

"Not yet," he replied. "But I know what you mean. The waiting is getting to me too. Over."

I could hear a motor running every time he pushed the talk button, so I figured he was out in his dad's shop in the garage. "What are you working on?" I asked. "Over."

"Just building a bug," he replied. "Over."

I was puzzled. "A bug? Over."

"An electronic homing device," he explained. "If we somehow get the chance to plant it on the kidnappers' car, it could lead us to Lisa! Over."

"Right," I replied. "And who's gonna stick it on the kidnappers' car? Do you know how dangerous that would be? What do you think Chief Ramsey would say if he knew you were even thinking of such a wild idea? Over."

"It's just an idea," he returned. "At least it gives me something to do while we wait. Over."

"Well, just forget about using it," I chided. "You could get yourself killed! Call me when you hear anything. Over and out."

"Will do," he promised. "Over and out."

I switched off the unit and lay down across the bed. I must have drifted off to sleep immediately. The next thing I knew, the walkie-talkie was beeping me awake. A glance at the clock told me that it was already four fifteen.

"Penny here," I answered. "Over."

"Chief Ramsey just called, Penny. The kidnappers called Mr. Diamond, giving him instructions to install a CB radio in his jeep. He's to be in the Diamond Computer parking lot at seven tonight with the money and the canvas top removed from the jeep. He'll get instructions by CB on where to drop off the ransom. Chief wants us at the house at six. Over."

"Stop by and pick me up," I replied. "Over."

"See ya, Penny. Over and out."

Sherlock and I reached the Diamonds' place early. Chief Ramsey was waiting for us. "We just finished getting the cash together," he said. "Larry just left for the Diamond complex with two agents discreetly tailing him in unmarked cars. We have a homing device planted on the jeep, which Larry doesn't know about, and we're going to attempt to tail him with unmarked cars and a helicopter. It's a slim chance, but perhaps we can pick up a trail on the kidnappers, and they'll lead us to Lisa."

We climbed into the police cruiser to wait. Fifteen minutes later a CB unit in the police car crackled to life. "Diamond? Listen carefully. Drive to the 69 northbound ramp, wait exactly three minutes, then head north. Got it?"

We heard Mr. Diamond's voice. "Yes, sir. 69 north. How far?" But the radio was silent, and he never got an answer.

Chief started the engine. "Let's roll!"

"What if the kidnappers see the police car?" I worried.

"Don't worry, Penny," Chief assured me. "We won't get that close. The unmarked cars will do the actual tailing. We're just going to try to stay within backup range in case we're needed."

We drove to within a mile or so of the Diamond building and then pulled into the parking lot of a convenience store. The radio crackled to life again. "Slow down, idiot! Wanna get pulled over?"

Then Mr. Diamond's voice. "Sorry."

We pulled out of the parking lot and headed north. I could hardly breathe. Every few minutes, new instructions came over the radio. Chief seemed to know exactly where they were and was driving an alternate route that would keep us fairly close but safely out of sight.

"Take the next gravel road to the right," the CB voice ordered. "When you get to the top of the ridge, stop in the middle of the road. Get out of the jeep and stand directly in front of it, facing the jeep."

We waited in silence. The voice came again. "Very good, Diamond. Now drop the suitcases over the ravine to your right, and drive on without looking back. Your daughter should be home tonight."

Suddenly the CB radio cursed violently. "Diamond, you idiot! We said no police! You may have just sacrificed your daughter's life!"

We heard Mr. Diamond. "What are you talking about? I came alone! Honest!" I knew he was telling the truth because he knew nothing of the police tail.

"There's a chopper in the air, rich boy, and it ain't the traffic watch! You just blew it, Diamond! Go back to your office until we decide what to do."

"Please, you've got to believe me," Mr. Diamond begged. "I knew nothing about it! Please! The money is there. You've got to believe me."

But the radio was silent.

Chief Ramsey picked up the mike. "Move in, men. Secure the money, and flag down Diamond. But don't, I repeat, do **not**, attempt to stop the suspects' vehicle!" He switched on the flashing lights on top of the cruiser and then gunned the powerful vehicle to a breathtaking speed.

He left the CB unit on in case of any further transmissions by the kidnappers but continued to talk on the police radio. "Bill! What's Larry Diamond's location?"

Officer Bill's voice answered immediately. "Somewhere in the Cave Creek game preserve, Chief. I tailed him to the entrance and then dropped back to let one of the FBI boys rotate in. He was heading up the road toward the fire break when I bowed out."

"How far in is he?" the chief questioned.

"Probably less than a mile," Officer Bill answered. "They ordered him to stop and drop the ransom less than ninety seconds after I left him."

Officer Clark came on. "I'm coming up on Diamond now, Chief. He's loading the suitcases back into his jeep. What do you advise?"

"Is the jeep blocking the road?" Chief Ramsey asked.

"Yes, sir."

"Good," the chief replied. "Listen carefully. The kidnappers may be nearby, and we want this to look right. Pull up behind the jeep and honk loudly, as if you're irritated that you can't get by. Get out and yell at Mr. Diamond, then head back to your car. Under your breath, tell him to back down and follow you.

"Remember the camping area at the entrance? Pull into one of the more secluded spots and then load the cash into your car as quickly as possible. Tell Diamond to return to his office complex. Bill, are you following my instructions to Clark?"

Officer Bill's voice replied, "Roger, sir."

"Good," Chief said. "Bill, head back into the game preserve and meet Clark at the campground, but keep your distance. Tail him back to the Diamonds' house, and we'll secure the ransom cash."

He glanced at us as he slammed his fist down on the steering wheel in disgust. "We shouldn't have used the chopper!" We did a quick U-turn and headed back the other direction. "Might as well head for the Diamonds'."

Sherlock sighed. "I was hoping we'd have Lisa safely home tonight."

"You weren't the only one," I lamented.

Clark's voice suddenly cut in, so excited he was shouting. "Chief! I just got a possible make on the kidnappers' car! White Ford Mustang, '01 or '02 model. License number LRJ740 or

748. Couldn't get close enough to tell without arousing suspicion. Two men in the car. They just cut in front of me from one of the old logging roads, and they were really moving."

"Good work, Clark," the chief responded. "I'll run a make on that license. Get down to that campground with Diamond and secure that money. We'll pick you up at the Diamonds'."

He called Mrs. Elgin, the dispatcher. "Run a make on a plate, number LRJ740, possibly 748. See if we have a white Mustang."

"Roger, Chief," Mrs. Elgin replied.

Just as we pulled into the Diamonds' driveway, she came back on. "Negative, Chief. LRJ740 is a '99 Cadillac. LRJ748 is a stolen plate."

I bit my lip. "Every lead we have just seems to fall flat, doesn't it?"

"Keep praying, Penny," Sherlock replied. I looked at him and nodded.

"I'll put out an APB on that license number," Chief Ramsey said, "with special instructions not to attempt to apprehend. Maybe someone will spot the plate, and we'll get lucky."

We met Officer Bill and Officer Clark back at the Diamond estate ten minutes later. Chief Ramsey helped the men carry the suitcases back into the house and set them on the kitchen floor. "Ever see a million dollars, Penny?"

Chief opened one of the larger suitcases, and my eyes grew wide at the sight of stacks and stacks of hundred-dollar bills. "No, thanks," I replied. "I think I'm happier being poor. At least I don't have to worry about being kidnapped."

Two hours later, Mr. Diamond's jeep pulled into the driveway. He hurried into the house carrying a portable tape recorder, and we clustered around him. His face was drawn and tight, and I could tell that the strain of the ordeal was wearing him down.

"A call just came to the office," he told Chief Ramsey, "and I thought you ought to hear it." He set the recorder on the kitchen table and switched it on.

"Diamond, you blew it!" the kidnapper's voice ranted. "You really blew it! We just buried the girl!"

NINE

THE WRECK

We stared at the recorder in horror as the tape continued to roll. The kidnapper laughed, and my blood ran cold. How could anyone be so heartless?

"Yes, sir, we buried her, Diamond," the voice continued, "but she's still alive—for now. Better listen closely. We buried your daughter underground in a shipping crate. You'll never find her without us. She has food and water. And she has air—for now. The batteries on the ventilation system we made will last about twenty-four hours. After that, well . . .

"We'll contact you in the morning for one last chance to redeem your daughter. Keep the two-point-four million handy. If you mess up this last time, we say goodbye for good. Got it? No more cops, Diamond!"

Mr. Diamond's voice was on the recording, pleading, fearful. "Wait! I didn't know about the police chopper. Honest! Can't we arrange something for tonight? Please? Lisa needs her insulin!"

But there was only a click and a dial tone. Chief Ramsey shut the recorder off.

Mr. Diamond sank to a chair, his head in his hands. "How do I tell my wife?" he asked helplessly. "The idea of Lisa buried in a box would terrify her. And what if we don't get to Lisa in time? It's been more than twenty-four hours since she's had her insulin!"

"Maybe she has it with her," I suggested hopefully, but he shook his head.

"Her purse was found on the floor of the limousine," he answered sadly. "She could be dead by now. How do we know that these wretched men are telling the truth?"

Chief Ramsey stepped close to Mr. Diamond and put a thick hand on his shoulder. "We just have to assume they're telling the truth, Larry," he said in a surprisingly gentle voice. "They'll contact you, as they promised. You'll get the money to them, and Lisa will be OK."

"But why wasn't I consulted about the chopper?" the millionaire demanded angrily. "It's my daughter's life at stake, and I don't even know what's going on! Lisa might be home by now if it hadn't been for that interfering helicopter!"

Chief Ramsey looked chastened. "I'm sorry, sir. We were figuring that your responses would be more natural if you didn't know that we were tailing you."

"I should have been consulted."

"I apologize, Mr. Diamond. We will make no more decisions of this nature without your knowledge."

The phone rang, and one of the agents took the call. "Diamond residence." He listened briefly, then said, "Thank you, Jim."

He turned to us. "We were unable to trace this last call."

Agent Meadows looked annoyed. "What happened?"

"We don't really know," the man replied. "When the connection was made, it was as though our equipment just dropped it."

Chief Ramsey ushered Sherlock and me to the door. "Better head for home, kids. It's going to be a long night, and there's no point in you staying. Might as well get some sleep."

That evening during supper I told Mom and Dad what had happened. "So Lisa's out there somewhere underground," I wailed. "She must be terrified! And the police still have no clue as to where she is. They don't even know who the kidnappers are."

Mom patted my arm. "God knows where she is, Penny. She's in His hands."

I tossed and turned all night, imagining the terror Lisa must have been feeling. I cried, and I prayed, and I worried. It was the worst night of my life.

The next morning Sherlock called me on the walkie-talkie. "I'm heading out to the Diamonds' house," he told me. "Care to come along? Over."

"Can you give me about twenty minutes? I haven't had breakfast yet. Over."

"Sure," he responded. "No hurry. But we've got a lot to do today. I want to check in with Chief, then if nothing's happening, I'd like to go out and interview Rick Dotson, the first man on the scene after the kidnapping. Maybe we can pick up some small clue. Penny, I've never been on any case that had so few leads. Over."

"See you in twenty minutes, Sherlock. Be praying for Lisa. Over and out."

Sherlock and I were pedaling toward town when he suddenly swerved to the side of the road and braked to a quick stop. Alarmed, I did the same, stopping about fifty feet ahead of him. "What's up?" I asked, puzzled.

"Maybe we just got our first break," he replied. "Follow me, but try to be as inconspicuous as possible."

We sauntered back along the road, and he stopped and pointed down an alley. "Look!"

Parked behind a vacant store was a fairly new white car. I looked at Sherlock. "So?"

"Penny, check the license number!"

"LRJ748," I read aloud, and then it sank in. "The license number of the kidnappers! That's the number Clark got yesterday in the game preserve."

"Maybe it's the kidnappers' car, maybe not," Sherlock responded. "Either way, we can't take a chance on losing it. Wait here, but get down behind this dumpster."

He ran back to his bike and took a small object from the bike basket, then crept down the alley. For a moment he knelt behind a trash can, studying the area. Once he was satisfied that all was clear, he ran to the back of the car, crouching as he ran. When he reached the car, he fell to the gravel, rolled over on his back, and then reached up underneath the car. *What on earth?* I thought. *He's going to get caught!*

At that moment, a door opened, and a man came walking toward the car. *Get out of there, Sherlock!* I thought desperately. But it was too late. Sherlock would never have time to run for it.

I held my breath. The man walked around the rear of the car, but Sherlock wasn't there! He had rolled completely under the car, out of sight of the man.

The stranger unlocked the driver's door, tossed in a package, and then relocked the door, glancing furtively around as he closed it. I ducked down, hoping that Sherlock would stay still. When I poked my head back up, the door to the building was just closing. I let out my breath. That was close!

Moments later, Sherlock crawled up beside me. "You just about got nailed!" I scolded in a whisper. "What on earth were you doing?"

"Just planting a bug," he replied with a grin.

"What?"

"If this is the kidnappers' car, we'll be able to follow it," he explained. "I planted my transmitter under the car. I have the receiver in my bike basket. Come on, we need to go get Chief Ramsey."

We reached the Diamond estate in record time. Chief Ramsey listened intently as we told him of finding the car. "Let's check it out," he said as we finished. He turned to an FBI agent. "Got an unmarked vehicle handy?"

The agent nodded. "I'll drive you." In moments the four of us were heading back toward the alley where we found the car.

"How's that thing work?" I asked Sherlock as we drove.

He shot an embarrassed glance at the men in the front seat, and then turned back to me. "It's actually quite primitive," he replied. "The meter on the face indicates the strength of the signal. The closer we get, the stronger the signal and the further the needle moves. By rotating the antenna, I can determine from which direction the signal originates. It's simple, but I think it will work."

The FBI agent was interested. "Where did you get that, son?"

Sherlock was embarrassed. "I made it, sir."

He glanced out the window. "We're almost there. Slow down." We cruised by the alley, but it was empty. The white car was gone.

The boy detective switched on the receiver in his hands. He rotated the little antenna on top, watching the meter as he did. "The signal's coming from behind us," he reported. "We need to turn around."

We cruised back the way we had come, with the agent following Sherlock's directions. In just moments he said, "I'm getting a really strong signal! We must be right on top of them!"

"There they are," Chief shouted. "To the right!"

I looked, and sure enough, there was the white Mustang, pulling out from a service station. Two men were in it, and I wondered if we were seeing Lisa's kidnappers for the first time. Cold chills ran up my back.

I turned to Sherlock. "If those are the kidnappers, then Irene Lewis wasn't involved."

He nodded. "Right."

"Back off," Chief Ramsey instructed the FBI man. "Give them plenty of room."

"You got it," the agent agreed.

Chief Ramsey got on the radio. "Requesting back up units," he said. "Following suspects eastbound on Main, approaching Third Street. Late model white Mustang, tag number LRJ748. Other units stay out of sight. Be ready to assume tail. Do not attempt to apprehend."

We followed the car all the way through town. The agent dropped back two or three blocks to make sure that we weren't spotted. Sherlock watched his homemade gadget closely to make sure we didn't lose the suspects.

As we left Willoughby behind, the suspects' car picked up speed. "Suspects eastbound at high rate of speed," Chief reported on the radio. "Do not attempt to apprehend."

"Uh oh," the agent said suddenly. "We've got trouble."

A sheriff's patrol car was sitting on the side of the highway with a radar unit hanging out the window. As the Mustang flashed past, the patrol car shot out onto the highway in pursuit, lights flashing.

"That idiot!" Chief Ramsey exploded. "He's going to blow this whole thing wide open!"

The appearance of the sheriff's car had an immediate effect. The Mustang shot ahead like a rock from a slingshot. "Hang on," the FBI agent muttered. "Here goes!" Our own car rocketed ahead.

"He's doing a hundred twenty already!" the agent reported.

Just then the Mustang pulled out to pass a string of slower cars. A curve loomed ahead, but the driver never slowed. "He's going to kill somebody," Sherlock whispered, his face white.

A logging truck swung into view, and the driver of the Mustang tried desperately to get back into his own lane. But the truck slammed head-on into the car, hurling the wreckage to the side of the highway. The truck careened across the highway, rocketed up a steep slope, then back down onto the shoulder of the highway, all without overturning.

The sheriff's car swerved onto the shoulder behind the wreckage of the Mustang, and the agent followed with our vehicle. The deputy sheriff climbed out of his car and started toward the Mustang, but Chief Ramsey warned him back. "Careful. They may be armed. They're suspects in a kidnapping."

The deputy drew his revolver and dropped behind the car. Chief turned back to us. "Stay in the car! We don't know what we'll find."

All three lawmen approached the demolished vehicle with guns drawn. They took one cautious look inside and then holstered their weapons. I knew instantly that there was no hope for the two men.

Sherlock and I watched from the back seat as the men checked the occupants of the car. The FBI agent withdrew the keys from the ignition and opened the trunk. After a quick glance inside, he closed it again.

Chief Ramsey leaned way into the Mustang, then withdrew his head and shoulder and walked back to our car. "They're both dead," he told us soberly. "Killed instantly. They won't be any help in finding Lisa now."

He held up a piece of jewelry. "This was on the floor in the back seat. Was it Lisa's?"

I looked at the gold bracelet dangling from his fingers and caught my breath. A diamond-studded heart swung from a fine gold chain. Engraved on the heart were the initials "LAD."

There was no longer any doubt that these were the men who had kidnapped Lisa. Now they were both dead, unable to give us a single clue as to Lisa's whereabouts. And Lisa was running out of time.

TEN

ONE SMALL CLUE

Officer Bill, Officer Clark, and the FBI men stood silently listening as Chief Ramsey told Mr. Diamond of the chase and the subsequent wreck. The millionaire took a deep breath and then let it out slowly.

"Perhaps they weren't the kidnappers," he said hopefully. "You said yourself that the license number was a stolen tag. We don't really know that they had anything to do with Lisa, just because Officer Clark spotted them in the game preserve yesterday."

I hated what I had to do, but I pulled the bracelet from my pocket. "Mr. Diamond," I whispered huskily. His eyes fell on the little item of jewelry, and his face turned white.

"Where . . . where did that come from?" he asked fearfully.

I handed it to him, and he took it with trembling fingers. "It . . . it was in the wrecked Mustang," I whispered, afraid to let my eyes meet his.

He sat back suddenly and sucked in his breath in a kind of moaning sob. He glanced at me, then at the bracelet, and then at Chief Ramsey. "Then they were the kidnappers," he said slowly.

He swung the bracelet gently back and forth and then dropped it into his pocket. He turned back to Chief as he asked, "What kind of leads do you have? How are we going to find Lisa?"

An uncomfortable silence prevailed as the entire group of lawmen looked at the floor. Mr. Diamond looked from one anxious face to another. "Well?"

Chief Ramsey spoke at last. "There's nothing, Larry. Not a single solitary clue. We checked the Mustang thoroughly, even going through the pockets of the kidnappers, but there was nothing to give us any information whatsoever."

Agent Meadows spoke up. "My men checked the vacant building where the kids first saw the car. Nothing."

"Are you telling me that Lisa is somewhere out there, imprisoned in a shipping crate, and no one knows how to go about finding her?"

"The only two people who knew where she is are now dead," Chief Ramsey said gently.

The millionaire looked hopefully at Sherlock. "What about it, son? Any ideas?"

Sherlock shook his head miserably, and Mr. Diamond burst into tears. "Oh Lisa, Lisa, Lisa," he sobbed. "Dear God, help me find my daughter!"

I hurt inside for him, imagining the grief he must be feeling. We all knew that Lisa would die unless someone could find her in time. The only people who had any idea where she was had died in the car wreck. *Dear God,* I prayed silently, *help us find her before it's too late!*

Mr. Diamond stood to his feet. "Excuse me please, gentlemen. I need a few minutes alone. If any of you know how to pray, please intercede for my Lisa right now and for our family."

As he slipped from the room, an idea suddenly occurred to me, and I turned to Sherlock. "What about Irene Lewis?" I asked hopefully. "Maybe she's involved in this. Maybe she hired the kidnappers to get revenge on Mr. Diamond! Maybe she knows where Lisa is."

Sherlock shook his head. "Miss Lewis had nothing to do with it," he sighed. "The two kidnappers were working on their own. They were after Mr. Diamond's money."

"But how do you know?" I argued, still unwilling to give up hope. "She's our only chance of finding Lisa!"

"Penny, we found a Willoughby city map in the glove compartment of the wrecked Mustang," Chief Ramsey told me. "It had three routes marked in red ink—the three possible routes that the Diamond limousine could have taken home from school. They marked the routes before they knew that Mr. Underwood always took Lisa home by the same route. We believe that the kidnappers were planning their crime before school even started."

Sherlock stepped over to the chief. "Sir, could I hear that last tape again? Perhaps we could pick up some sort of clue . . ." His voice trailed off.

The lawman shrugged. "There's nothing on there that will help, Sherlock."

"But we've got to do something, sir," my friend protested. He glanced at his watch. "If the kidnapper was right, Lisa has less than eight hours!"

Chief Ramsey nodded. "It couldn't hurt." He turned to an agent. "Get me the tape, would you?"

My anxiety grew as we listened to the tape again. "Diamond, you blew it!" the kidnapper's voice ranted. "You really blew it! We just buried the girl!"

Then there was that awful, heartless laughter.

"Yes, sir, we buried her, Diamond," the voice continued, "but she's still alive—for now. Better listen closely. We buried your daughter underground in a shipping crate. You'll never find her without us. She has food and water. And she has air—for now. The batteries on the ventilation system we designed will last for about twenty-four hours. After that, well . . ."

"We'll contact you in the morning for one last chance to redeem your daughter. Keep the two-point-four million handy. If you mess up this last time, we say goodbye for good. Got it? No more cops, Diamond!"

And then, Mr. Diamond's voice again. "Wait! I didn't know about the police chopper. Honest! Can't we arrange something for tonight? *Please?* Lisa needs her insulin!"

Sherlock frowned. "May I rewind it?" He rewound the tape and listened to it again, then a third time.

Agent Meadows spoke up. "There's nothing on there, boy. We listened to it half a dozen times. Like everything else these guys did, they left absolutely no clues!"

But I had seen Sherlock's eyes light up like they always do when he's on to something. I held my breath. "Pick up on something?"

He shook his head. "I don't know. Listen to this." He rewound the tape, played the part that said "after that well . . ." then paused the tape. He leaned forward. "Now, listen closely."

Sherlock released the pause button.

"We'll contact you in the morning for one more chance to redeem your daughter."

He pushed the pause button. "Did you hear it?"

I frowned. "Hear what?"

Sherlock shook his head. "I don't know. There's a strange background noise every time I play that one sentence, but I can't make out what it is."

"Turn the volume up and play it again," Agent Meadows suggested.

Sherlock did, and the men clustered eagerly around the table. "Rewind it and play it again, son."

Officer Bill nodded. "I think I hear what you're talking about," he said. "It starts right after the word 'contact'."

"That's it," Sherlock agreed, "but what's the noise? If we turn it up louder, then the static and other noises get louder also."

"We could have the tape 'cleaned up' electronically," Agent Meadows suggested. He looked at the other agents. "What do you think? Is it worth pursuing?"

"What other clues do we have?" Officer Clark remarked. "I say go for it."

I looked at Sherlock. "What are they talking about?"

"The tape can be played through special electronic filters which erase all sounds but those in a certain frequency range," Sherlock explained. "It's done by computer. We would try to select the sound frequency that this noise is on and then remove all other sounds. If it works, we might be able to make out what this sound is."

"Why is that so important?" I asked.

"Maybe we could figure out where this call originated," Agent Meadows replied. "Perhaps we could pick up some small clue. Anything. Right now we're grasping at straws."

He turned to one of the agents. "Get on the phone and find a studio that has the equipment. Once you locate one, make sure they move this through as a priority one."

The man was back in ten minutes. "There's a studio down in Griswold that can handle it," he reported. "That's about thirty miles from here. They say it'll take at least an hour to do the tape."

Agent Meadows jumped to his feet. "Let's move!" He grabbed the recorder and turned to Chief Ramsey. "Come with Agent Lewis and me, Chief. You know this area better than we do."

He looked at Sherlock. "How about you and the girl coming along for the ride? You're in on this too." After two quick phone calls to get permission from our parents, Sherlock and I were speeding toward Griswold.

"Do you think you'll learn anything, once the tape is cleaned up?" I asked Sherlock.

"Don't get your hopes up, young lady," Meadows told me. "It's probably nothing. But right now, we're ready to try anything."

Once we reached the studio, Agent Meadows persuaded the manager to put a technician on the project immediately. The man listened as Sherlock explained what we needed and played the one sentence.

The technician laughed. "Just that short segment, huh? That shouldn't take fifteen minutes." He disappeared with the tape.

Twenty minutes later he handed us our tape, plus another cassette. "Here it is," he told us, "but I do hope you're not too disappointed. I'm afraid you didn't get much."

Sherlock popped the new tape into the cassette player and turned it on.

"Welcome to Burger Bob's," a female voice said in metallic tones. "May I take your order?"

ELEVEN

THE PAY PHONE

I stared at the tape recorder in dismay. All that work and effort for this: "Welcome to Burger Bob's"?

But Sherlock was ecstatic. "That's it!" he cried. "Burger Bob's! The call originated from the phone booth near the Burger Bob's restaurant drive-thru!"

"Yeah, but which one?" Agent Meadows muttered. "It could take two days to check all the Burger Bob's in the state."

Sherlock shook his head. "The Burger Bob's in Spencerville is right next door to the Big Value hardware store. And there's a pay phone at the end of the parking lot, right beside the kerosene tank."

"I can't believe you'd notice a detail like that," I remarked.

Sherlock shrugged. "I try to be observant."

"Then let's scramble," Chief Ramsey declared. He opened his wallet and withdrew a business card, handing it to the manager of the sound studio. "Send me a statement, would you? We're dealing with an emergency."

The manager shook his head. "No charge."

As we raced for Spencerville, the chief radioed the base at the Diamond house. "Clark, bring a couple of agents and meet us at the Burger Bob's in Spencerville. Have them bring a finger-print kit. There's a small chance we may have a lead."

When we pulled into the parking lot of the hardware store twenty minutes later, I saw that Sherlock was right. There was a pay phone—one of those little jobs on a pole with a small hood around it—at the far end of the parking lot. In fact, it was less than thirty feet from the speaker of the restaurant drive-thru menu board!

Clark was waiting for us. He and two men got out of a car in the Burger Bob's lot and met us at the end of the Big Value parking lot. "We believe that the last call originated from this phone," Agent Meadows told them. "Dust the phone and the minibooth for prints."

He turned back to Chief Ramsey. "Would it be a local call to the Diamonds' place from here?"

The chief nodded. "I'm sure it would."

The FBI man looked disappointed. "Then we can't trace the billing on the call," he said.

"Welcome to Burger Bob's!" a voice behind me said, and I jumped. "May I take your order?" I laughed and relaxed as I realized that a car had pulled up to the menu board and the oc-cupants were preparing to order. "Sounds like the same girl we heard on the tape," I told Sherlock.

One of the agents dusted a fine white powder on the phone and the blue fiberglass shell of the little booth. He took several minutes to examine the entire booth carefully and then used pieces of transparent tape to make a record of several fingerprints.

He placed the tape over the print he wanted and lifted it carefully. The fingerprints stuck to the tape.

Pounding rock music began to blare, and I turned in disgust. A convertible with three teenagers was approaching the menu board. "They always have to play it so that you can hear it two blocks away," I remarked to Sherlock.

"Yes, but they'll suffer severe hearing loss as a result," he replied. The noise subsided somewhat as the car pulled forward after ordering.

The FBI agent had finished his work on the phone. "Three usable prints, sir," he reported to Agent Meadows when he was finished. "Two thumbs and an index finger."

"Fine, but where does that get us?" Meadows replied. "We already know who made the call." He turned to Sherlock. "Pick up any clues?"

Sherlock just shook his head miserably.

As we headed for our cars, Sherlock looked at his watch. "Six-and-a-half hours," he remarked quietly. I knew all too well what the countdown was.

As the agent started the car, Sherlock suddenly jerked upright. "Wait for me," he told the man. "I have an idea."

I followed him back to the phone. "What's your idea?" I asked, but apparently, he was too preoccupied to hear me. He seized the phone book and began to page through the white pages. "What are you looking for, Sherlock?" But he still didn't hear me.

He was in the "D" section of the book. "Daisy Inn," he murmured, reading the heading at the top of the page. He dropped his finger to the lower right corner. "Diagnostic. Almost there."

As he fumbled to turn the page, I suddenly realized what he was searching for. "You won't find Diamond in there," I told him. "They've just been in town a few months. They won't be listed yet."

He gave me an impatient look. "Penny, I know that." As he turned the page, his face lit up, and I knew he had found whatever it was he was looking for. "Pay dirt! Look, Penny!"

His skinny finger was pointing to the top of the new page, where two phone numbers were written in ink. I shrugged. "So what?"

"So what?" He was so excited he was almost shouting. "Penny, this is the number for Diamond Computer! This was written by one of the kidnappers."

"So what's the other number?"

"I don't know, but we're about to find out." He was fishing in his pocket. "Got any change?" I shook my head, and he raced for the car. When he returned, the three men were close on his heels.

Sherlock plunked coins into the phone and then dialed the second number with trembling fingers. He waited a moment, and then said, "Yes. Can you tell me where you're located?"

And then, "Very well. Thank you." He hung up and threw a fist into the air. "Yes!"

We all stared at him. "What was that number?" I asked.

"Spencerville Rent-All," he answered. "They rent tools and equipment. We may just be onto something." He turned to Agent Lewis. "They're about two miles from here," he said, "on the Boulevard. We need to take a left at the next stop sign."

The agent nodded. "Let's go!"

We scrambled for the car.

I bowed my head in the back seat. "Lord, we've been disappointed so many times so far," I prayed. "Please, not again. Lisa is just about out of time!"

TWELVE

THE RENTAL AGENCY

Sherlock and I sat impatiently in the back seat with Chief Ramsey as Agent Lewis drove toward the rental agency. Traffic was terrible. We pulled up to the stop sign behind six other cars. And every one of them had its turn signal on, waiting to turn left into the bustling traffic on the boulevard. I groaned. This would take forever.

Chief Ramsey pointed to a big gold-colored car in front of us. "Look at that old Cadillac," he said. "I think it's a '78 model."

"The driver's an antique too," Agent Meadows cracked. "I'll bet she's the original owner."

I leaned forward to see. A tiny head covered with white curls showed just above the back of the front seat of the Cadillac. The woman reminded me of Mrs. Peabody.

I turned to Sherlock. "How did you know to look in the phone book for that number?" I asked. "You said you knew that

Diamond Computer wouldn't be in there, so why did you even look?"

Sherlock shrugged. "I guess the idea came from the Lord," he replied. "He seemed to be telling me to go back to the phone booth."

"But you knew that Diamond wasn't listed in the book yet," I persisted, "so why did you look?"

"What do you do when a phone number isn't in the book? You call Directory Assistance and then write the number down. I figured that perhaps the kidnapper had done the same. He looked up Diamond Computer Technology, found it wasn't listed, and then called Directory Assistance. When he called Directory Assistance, he asked for the numbers for Diamond and for the rental place and wrote them both down."

"Come on, lady, come on," Agent Lewis muttered. "We haven't got all day!"

I looked up. The ancient Cadillac was the only vehicle in front of us now. A moderate break appeared in the traffic, and the big car inched forward about a foot and then stopped again.

"She's going to wait until the street is completely empty," the agent complained. "We'll be here all day."

I felt as impatient as our driver did. Maybe we finally had a clue as to Lisa's whereabouts, and I was dying to find out! I glanced at Sherlock, and I could tell that he was growing impatient too.

Another break appeared in the traffic, but the Cadillac still didn't move. The agent honked gently. "Come on, come on!" he sputtered.

When the third break appeared and the elderly lady still hadn't taken advantage of it, cars behind us began to honk. I tried to still my rising impatience. I was chafing to get to that rental place, and it looked like this lady would never move!

The woman let a fourth, fifth, and sixth break go by, and Chief Ramsey opened the back door. "Enough of this," he growled, pulling a pair of white gloves and a whistle from the pocket of his uniform.

While we watched in amazement, Chief strode purposefully to the center of the busy Boulevard, dodging cars the entire time. He blew a long blast on the whistle, held up both white-gloved hands, and brought the traffic to a stop. Then walking to within twenty feet of the old Cadillac, he motioned for the woman to proceed.

The Cadillac slowly made a cautious left turn, and Chief Ramsey motioned for us to proceed also. The agent turned left and then pulled over to the right curb to wait for Chief. But Chief stayed in the center of the street until every car on the side street had gone. I counted twenty-three cars after ours.

Chief Ramsey walked to our side of the Boulevard, blew his whistle, and then waved for the traffic to continue. The agents were laughing as he climbed into the car. "That uniform's good for something, isn't it, Chief?" one of them jested.

We hurried toward the rental agency, passing several slower cars. Sherlock leaned forward. "There it is, up ahead on the left," he said, pointing to a large yellow sign. "Spencerville Rent-All."

Spencerville Rent-All was one of those places where you could rent almost anything you wanted, from silverware to tractors. A huge fenced lot in the back contained a vast assortment of power equipment, while the spacious showroom displayed items for use inside one's home. We parked and hurried inside.

A tall, thin college student with a bad case of acne was behind the counter. We got in line behind two other customers. When our turn came, one of the FBI agents stepped forward.

"We need information concerning a rental that was made yesterday," he said pleasantly, "to a David Hayes or Victor Rodriguez."

The clerk frowned and shook his head. "We don't disclose that type of information," he said belligerently.

The agent flipped open his wallet and displayed a badge. "FBI business," he said.

But the man just folded his arms across his chest. "I'm very sorry, gentlemen, but we don't disclose that type of information."

Chief Ramsey leaned across the counter. "A young girl's life is at stake," he declared. "And your information could help her. Time is running out."

"Gentlemen, I wish I could help," the rental clerk replied. "But I don't think I'm at liberty to just pass out that sort of information. Not without a court order or something."

I sighed deeply. How were we going to convince this guy to give us the information we so desperately needed?

"Look," one of the agents told the clerk, "we can get a court order, if needed. But that will take time, and while we wait, a young girl could be dying! Now how about a little help?"

"You'll have to talk to my manager," the clerk replied.

"How do we reach him?" the agent asked.

"He's out on the equipment lot."

"You could have told us that at the beginning," Chief Ramsey snarled as he hurried for the side door.

We stepped out onto a paved lot filled with a vast array of tools and equipment. Cement mixers, engine hoists, ditch digging rigs, and even small bulldozers were all standing at attention, ready to be rented. We hurried down the rows of equipment toward a fat man with a clipboard.

"Agent Meadows, FBI," the agent said, displaying his badge. "We're on an emergency case, and time is of the essence. Can you tell us if a David Hayes or a Victor Rodriguez rented tools or equipment yesterday, probably late afternoon?"

"I'd have that in the rental files," the man said pleasantly. "Follow me."

The manager flipped through a stack of rental cards while the arrogant clerk eyed us uneasily. "Here it is," the manager said, holding up a card. "They rented a small backhoe. Returned it just before we closed last night at nine."

"Is the machine here now?" Chief Ramsey inquired.

"We passed it on the way in."

"Could we take a look at it?'

"Certainly."

We followed him back out to the equipment lot and stopped at a yellow machine that looked like a large garden tractor with a big, jointed arm at the back end and a large scoop at the end of the arm. The scoop had several large, steel teeth along one end. I would have loved to dig sandcastles at the beach with that rig!

"This is it, gentlemen," the manager said. "How may I be of further assistance?"

"We'd just like to look it over, if you don't mind," Chief Ramsey said, and the manager nodded obligingly.

"Help yourself. I'll be over by the sandblasters. Holler if you have any questions." He turned and walked toward the back of the lot.

The three men swarmed eagerly around the machine, but Sherlock stepped over to the scoop on the back. He glanced inside the scoop, then whipped out a handkerchief and a pocket-knife. Scraping a chunk of yellowish-brown dirt from one of the big steel teeth, he caught it in his handkerchief, then broke the chunk open, and examined it closely. I saw a number of transparent crystals mixed with a chalky yellowish-white mineral.

"Chief! Look at this!"

Chief Ramsey hurried to him. "What is it, son?"

Sherlock showed him the chunk of dirt. "It's selenite!" he said excitedly. "Crystallized gypsum! Lisa must be buried somewhere close to a gypsum mine!"

He turned and dashed after the stocky manager, and we hurried after him. "Sir," he asked breathlessly, "is there a gypsum mine anywhere in this area?"

The man turned and looked at him strangely. "Not in this region, son," he answered. "There's probably not a single gypsum mine within two hundred miles of here."

Sherlock's shoulders sagged.

"The last mine around here closed down years ago."

Sherlock's head snapped up. "Where?" he begged. "Where was the mine?"

The man ran a chubby hand across his face. "There's an abandoned gypsum mine out on Shallowford Pike," he replied. "Probably twelve or fourteen miles from here. I used to hunt doves there with my dad."

Chief Ramsey spoke up. "How do we get there, sir? It's important!"

The man took a sheet from his clipboard, turned it over, and then began to write on the back. "I'll just sketch out a little map," he said.

Ninety seconds later we were scrambling back into the car to begin a wild race against time.

THIRTEEN

DESPERATE SEARCH

A sudden thought occurred to me as Agent Lewis drove rapidly toward Shallowford Pike, and I turned to Sherlock. "If the kidnappers buried Lisa before they called Mr. Diamond, why did they call the rental place after they called him?"

Sherlock smiled. "Why do you say they called the rental place after they called him?"

"Because," I reasoned, "if they had called the rental place first, they would have looked it up in the book rather than getting it from Directory Assistance. They looked for Diamond Computer in the book first, and when they didn't find it, called Directory Assistance for both numbers."

He smiled again. "Good thinking, Penny," he congratulated me. "You'll make a good detective after all." He then went on to say, "I don't believe Lisa was buried when they called Mr. Diamond. They probably had the shipping crate and ventilation system ready and decided to call Mr. Diamond when they called to locate the equipment to dig with."

He looked thoughtful. "The Lord was in it though. If they had called at any other time, we wouldn't have been able to link them to the rental store."

The car slowed for a turn, and Agent Lewis spoke up. "How far did he say this place would be?"

"Twelve to fourteen miles," Chief Ramsey answered.

"We're just turning onto Shallowford Pike now," Agent Lewis said, looking at the odometer, "and we've come almost exactly two miles. Ten or twelve miles should get us there." We were now on the outskirts of town, and there was no traffic. So he stepped on the accelerator, and the car shot forward. We must have been doing eighty.

A short while later he reported, "We're nearing the twelve-mile point, so keep an eye out. We should be getting close."

We were on a lonely, desolate stretch of road and hadn't seen a house or farm for several miles. Gently rolling hills on both sides were dotted with occasional clusters of pine trees, and there were open areas with tall weeds and bushes, but the forests were gone. "This area was heavily strip-mined in the fifties and sixties," Chief Ramsey observed, "but there was no reclamation done to speak of. The scars are still here."

Agent Lewis was looking at the map that the rental manager had drawn. "We've already done eighteen miles, and I haven't seen any sign of an abandoned gypsum mine. It should have been on the left."

My heart sank. What if we couldn't even find the place?

The car slowed, and he made a U-turn. "Let's retrace the last two or three miles. We must have missed it."

Moments later Sherlock leaned forward. "There," he said, pointing, "on the right. That could be it, couldn't it?"

Agent Lewis pulled to the side of the road, stopping about ten feet from the four-strand barbed wire fence that ran along the shoulder. A rutted lane leading away from the road was barely visible in the tall grass. "What makes you think that could be it, Sherlock?" Chief asked.

"Those power poles," Sherlock replied, pointing. A row of decaying poles angled away from the road to meet the lane at the point where it disappeared over a gentle rise. "They carried some fairly heavy voltage."

The men looked at each other. "What do you think?"

A door opened, and Sherlock was out of the car and over at the fence before I realized he was gone. He was back at the car in seconds, his eyes shining with excitement. "The fence has been cut recently," he reported, "and patched back together with new wire! Can we check it out?"

We scrambled from the car to check it out. While the men were examining the fence, I spotted something white behind a tall clump of brush and went to take a look. I bent back a leafy branch to find a small, metal sign reading, "Leased to Davis Mining Co. NO TRESPASSING!"

I called Sherlock over and showed him. "It's mining property all right," he agreed. "Now to find out if it's the right one."

Apparently he saw the worried look on my face. "I think this is it, Penny," he assured me. "Someone messed with that fence just in the last day or two. The new pieces of wire haven't corroded in the least."

Agent Lewis brought a pair of wire cutters from the trunk of the car, and in moments, we were driving across the field, following the ancient road. I let out my breath slowly. Were we about to find Lisa? Would she still be alive? I prayed fervently.

The car topped the rise, and Agent Lewis stopped. All five of us sat silently staring at the abrupt change in the terrain. An ugly gash in the earth nearly half a mile wide stretched in front of us to disappear over the hills in the distance. All vegetation had been stripped away, leaving the reddish-yellow soil exposed. Here and there an occasional weed dotted the barren landscape. I've never been to the desert, but the scene before us reminded me of pictures I've seen of the desert in New Mexico.

Just off to our right was a huge pit several hundred yards wide and so deep we couldn't even see the bottom from where we sat. Several rusting metal shacks perched on the edge of the pit partially hidden by mounds of yellow dirt. An old truck and two earthmovers sat forlornly, abandoned when the mine closed.

Agent Meadows sighed loudly. "It could take us a week to search this place," he remarked. "Any suggestions?"

Sherlock was already out of the car. "Let's check for tracks." He bent down, examining the dusty roadway, and then straightened up almost immediately. "Fresh tracks!" he announced. "Made within the last day or two!"

I was at his side in a moment. "How can you tell?" I questioned. I noticed sparkling crystals in the soil, like the ones we had seen in the chunk of dirt from the backhoe.

"Notice how sharp and detailed the tracks are," he replied. "This soil is so dry and so fine that the wind would obliterate any tracks within just a few days."

"The boy's right," Agent Meadows agreed, kneeling to take a closer look. "These tracks were made within the last day or so."

Sherlock walked down the gentle slope, examining the roadway carefully, and I followed along. The three men got back in the car, and Agent Lewis let the car coast slowly along behind us. At the bottom of the slope, the road curved to the left. Sherlock got excited. "They're towing a trailer," he announced. "Two axles."

I frowned. "How can you tell?"

He pointed to the tracks. "When any vehicle makes a turn, the tracks widen slightly, as the back wheels do not follow exactly in the tracks of the front wheels. These tracks get even wider, as the trailer wheels stray even further from the tracks of the car."

Chief Ramsey was out of the car, examining the tracks. "You're right, son; it was a trailer. An equipment trailer loaded with a small backhoe perhaps?"

Sherlock nodded. "That's what I'm thinking."

But the road was heavily graveled further on, and we lost the tracks completely. Four of us got out and searched on foot while Agent Lewis cruised slowly behind us, but it was as though the vehicle had vanished into thin air.

Chief Ramsey finally called a halt. "It's going to be dark in about three hours," he said. "It could take us three days to search this place, and Lisa doesn't have that much time. We better call in some help."

Agent Meadows switched on the radio and picked up the mike. "Agent Wilson, come in, please. Meadows here." He called several more times, but there was no answer.

Chief Ramsey stepped forward. "Let me try to raise one of my officers." He switched to the Willoughby police frequency and tried, but he got the same results. Finally he turned to Agent Meadows. "We're out of range."

The FBI man frowned. "We couldn't be."

Chief shrugged. "There may be some interference from a magnetic field or something else blocking the signal. But at any rate, we're not getting through. Why don't you four continue to search, and I'll take the car back into town to call. We need to get some help here as fast as possible."

Agent Lewis spoke up. "How are they going to find us? We had a hard enough time. They'll drive right by it."

"Do you have any emergency flares in the trunk?" Sherlock asked. "You could leave those in the road to mark the spot when you return."

The agent nodded. "Good thinking. There's at least three or four flares beside the spare tire."

Chief Ramsey took off in the car, and we continued to search. We spread out in a straight line with each person about fifty feet from the next, carefully examining the ground for tire tracks or evidence of digging. I grew uneasy, realizing how long it would take to search this whole area. We'd never find Lisa in time.

Chief Ramsey was back in about twenty-five minutes. "I got through," he reported to Agent Meadows. "Your men are on their way down along with Mr. Diamond. I left four thirty-minute flares in the road, as well as a fluorescent safety vest hanging on the fence. They should be able to find us with no problem."

"It won't be any too soon," the FBI man replied. "I figure we've got about two-and-a-half hours of daylight left."

Some time later I glanced up to see a Willoughby police cruiser make its way down the slope, followed by two more vehicles. Officer Bill and Officer Clark leaped out of the police car, and eleven FBI agents scrambled from the other cars. Agent Meadows gathered them for instructions.

"Five of you inspect the buildings and the quarry pit," he said, "While the rest of us continue to walk a grid. We don't have much time!"

"Mr. Diamond should be here shortly," Officer Bill informed him. "He was going to round up some of his employees."

We spread out again in a longer chain this time. Sherlock was to my right, and Officer Bill was to my left. I prayed as we walked. My shoes filled up with sand and dust, but there was no time to stop and empty them. Time was running out.

I swatted at the gnats buzzing around my head and then knelt to examine the ground beneath a clump of bushes. A strange buzzing sound filled the air, and I paused, listening. What in the world?

I sucked in my breath sharply. Coiled directly in front of me, less than two feet from my knees, was a large rattlesnake! The rattles on his tail were vibrating so fast I could hardly see them. I didn't dare move. *Lord, help me!* I prayed silently.

FOURTEEN

VOLUNTEERS

My heart seemed to stop for a few seconds as I crouched face to face with the dangerous reptile. My chest tightened in fear, and my head began to pound. I couldn't even breathe. Black spots swam before my eyes, and I realized that I was in danger of passing out. If I fell, the rattlesnake would strike instantly.

Lord, help me! I prayed silently. I breathed slowly, deeply, until my racing heart had slowed somewhat.

I began to turn my head slowly to search for Sherlock or Officer Bill, but apparently the snake detected the movement. The angry buzzing increased in tempo, and I held perfectly still. I didn't dare even move my eyes.

"Penny, what did you find?" Sherlock's voice cut through the dark fog of my fear, and I welcomed the sound of it. At least I was not alone.

But then a new fear surged through me. If Sherlock approached, the snake would strike! But I also knew better than to call out. I prayed hard.

"Penny, have you got something?" The voice was closer this time, much closer. I winced but didn't dare turn my head to see how close. "What did you—oh my!" I knew he had spotted the rattlesnake, and relief washed over me. He would know better than to get too close.

"Penny, stay still," he ordered. "I'll get Officer Bill."

Moments later I heard Sherlock shouting in the distance. "Officer Bill! We need you! Rattlesnake!"

It was probably just a few seconds, but it seemed like hours before I heard Officer Bill's voice. "I'm to your left, Penny, about thirty feet from you. I'm going to move in closer and shoot the snake. Slowly close your eyes, but don't move." I heard a small click as he cocked his revolver.

Sweat ran down my neck, and the gnats buzzing around my head were having a ball. I slowly closed my eyes, but I didn't dare move anything else. I heard Officer Bill's voice again. "Wait for my shot, Penny. Then throw yourself over in a backward somersault, away from the snake. Ready? Here goes!"

The revolver blast was as loud as a cannon. I lunged backwards then scrambled to my feet and dashed away as fast as I could. I tripped and fell face down in the dirt and then realized that I still had my eyes closed. The gun roared again.

I spun around and opened my eyes. Officer Bill was standing with his revolver pointed at the writhing body of the snake. "Got him," he announced happily. "Took his head right off!"

"Thanks," I said shakily. "I thought I was a goner!"

Officer Bill slipped his revolver into its holster. "Glad to do it," he grinned. "Now, we had better get busy again."

"Look!" Sherlock exclaimed. Officer Bill and I spun around and looked in the direction he pointed. Cars, trucks, and SUVs were winding their way down the dusty road toward us. There must have been thirty vehicles!

We ran toward them, and I recognized Mr. Diamond in the lead car. He rolled down the window as we approached. "Find anything?"

Officer Bill shook his head. "Not yet," he replied.

The millionaire sighed deeply. "She doesn't have much time left."

Sherlock stepped close to the car. "Mr. Diamond, this is the right place. We're going to find her. I know it!"

Mr. Diamond nodded. "Thanks, Sherlock."

Car doors slammed and people came hurrying over. There were dozens of men and women of all ages and even a few teens and children. I watched in astonishment. "Who are all of these people?"

"Diamond employees and their families," Mr. Diamond answered. "They came to help search for Lisa." His voice broke.

Chief Ramsey came hurrying over. "Let's get these folks organized," he told Mr. Diamond. Raising his voice, he called, "Gather over here for instructions! There's no time to lose!"

The crowd gathered in close, and I noticed many of them carrying rakes and shovels. "We need to string out in a search pattern," Chief Ramsey instructed. "Thirty feet between you and the next person. Look for tire tracks, signs of digging, or even some type of ventilation hose. We have to find Lisa tonight, and we have less than two hours of daylight. Ready? Let's fan out. I'll get you organized."

Mr. Diamond spoke up. "May I say something?"

Chief nodded. "Of course."

"I appreciate each one of you coming," the millionaire said, tears forming in his eyes. "Lisa is special to Dana and me, and we're grateful for your help." He wiped a tear away and then continued.

"There's a lot of ground to cover, and there's not much time. We need all the help we can get." He paused, and a few people moved in closer.

"As every one of you knows, I'm a Christian. Lisa is too, and I'm thankful she's in God's hands. God knows where she is. Let's bow and ask Him to guide us to her, shall we?"

I couldn't help crying as I listened to this tall, wealthy man humbly ask God to guide the searchers. And as he prayed, my own faith grew. If Mr. Diamond could trust God, why couldn't I?

I knew that many of the Diamond employees were unsaved, and yet Mr. Diamond had prayed right in front of them. Surely God would answer, if only to demonstrate to the unbelievers that He could do it!

Chief Ramsey positioned the line of volunteers with each searcher about ten yards from the next. The line stretched almost completely across the bare earth of the old mine! We walked slowly, heads down, scanning the ground intently. Occasionally some one would call out, and the line would pause hopefully while some possibility was carefully examined. Twice we found fresh tire tracks, but both times they disappeared again within a few yards. In an hour, we were nearly a mile from the road.

I looked at the sky. Maybe an hour until it would get dark. We had to hurry!

I heard a shout from a little old lady about four or five people down the line. "I've found something!"

A number of us went scurrying over, Sherlock and me included. The lady had been probing the ground beneath a bush and had spotted a piece of blue plastic. Sherlock was on his knees in a flash, scrambling under the thorny branches.

Almost immediately he backed out, stood up, and seized the bush with both hands. He tugged, and the bush came out of the ground easily. Two small blue hoses about three inches in diameter were now visible.

Sherlock let out a shout. "We found it! This is it! Chief Ramsey! We found it!" Voices chattered excitedly as dozens of searchers came hurrying over.

Now that the bush was gone, a square of freshly turned earth was visible. Sherlock knelt and put an ear to the end of one of the ventilation hoses. "I hear a fan running! We're in time!" The crowd went wild. Cheers and shouts were mingled with tears.

Mr. Diamond came rushing up, his eyes brimming with tears. He knelt and shouted down one of the tubes, "Lisa, it's Daddy! Can you hear me?"

He stood to his feet. "I can't hear anything! Please, be quiet!" The crowd immediately grew silent.

"Lisa!" he called again. "Can you hear me? It's Daddy!"

He leaped to his feet and grabbed a shovel from a nearby volunteer. "She doesn't answer!" he shouted in anguish, stabbing at the ground with the shovel. "She doesn't answer! Somebody help me dig!"

FIFTEEN

THE BUTTERFLY

Mr. Diamond dug frantically at the loose soil. "Help me!" he cried. "We have to get her out!"

Chief Ramsey came dashing up. "Move back!" he instructed the throng of volunteers, who were crowding so close that they were in danger of being hit with Mr. Diamond's shovel. "Give us room!" The onlookers moved back obediently.

"You there," he said, pointing to a strong-looking man, "start digging. And you." He chose another man. He grabbed a shovel from the hands of a third and started digging himself. "There's room for four of us to dig without being in each other's way," he said. "You others can relieve us if it becomes necessary."

The crowd remained silent as the four shovels bit into the earth time after time. The two hoses in the ground hindered the men as they tried not to damage them. But the soil was soft, and the hole grew rapidly. Within two minutes, the hole was nearly eighteen inches deep. "One of the hoses is collapsed," a spectator observed, and a groan went up from the crowd. The earth around one of the hoses had caved in, squashing the flexible tube nearly flat. The men with the shovels worked even faster.

"I hit something!" Mr. Diamond exclaimed, and the onlookers pushed forward. "Something hard!"

He dropped his shovel and began to scoop away the dirt with his hands. He uncovered a plastic garbage bag, which he lifted, exposing a car battery. Two wires ran from the battery terminals into the ground.

The millionaire seized the battery and hefted it out of the hole, jerking the two wires loose. He hurled the heavy battery to one side. "Dig!" he pleaded, seizing his own shovel and working frantically. A moment later, we heard a solid "thunk" as one of the shovels hit a piece of wood.

The men quickly cleared the dirt away, revealing a piece of plywood about three feet square. They pried at the edges of the wood with their shovels, but the plywood refused to budge. "Here, Mr. Diamond," a spectator said, handing the man a crowbar, "use this!"

Mr. Diamond knelt in the hole and inserted the claw of the crowbar under the edge of the plywood. He pried with all this strength. With a groan of protesting nails, the plywood lifted about two inches. Chief Ramsey and another man inserted their shovels and helped him pry the plywood up several more inches.

Mr. Diamond dropped his crowbar and seized the edge of the plywood in both muscular hands. Gritting his teeth with the effort, he pulled the plywood free, stepping out of the hole as he did. The lid was off. A small fan was fastened to the underside of the lid, directly beneath the hole leading to one of the ventilation tubes.

The entire crowd pressed forward. We could now see that the box was about three-and-a-half feet deep. Slumped in one corner, with her head down and her knees drawn up to her chin, was Lisa Diamond. Her left hand clutched a flashlight. A gallon jug of water, two apples, half a loaf of bread, and a roll of toilet paper lay at her feet.

"Lisa, it's Daddy!" Mr. Diamond exclaimed, but Lisa didn't move.

Mr. Diamond jumped into the crate and seized his daughter by the arms, lifting her to the waiting hands above him. The men gently deposited the limp body on the ground, and I saw Lisa's face for the first time. Her eyes were closed, and her skin was a pale, grayish color. My heart seemed to leap into my throat. We were too late!

But Officer Bill knelt beside her, his ear to her mouth, two fingers pressed to the side of her throat. "She's alive," he announced, "but barely."

"Here, Bill!" I looked up to see Officer Clark pushing his way through the crowd with a small green oxygen cylinder in his hand. He knelt beside Lisa and placed a transparent green mask over her face, then opened a valve on the cylinder.

"Let's get her into the patrol car," he said. I looked up to see one of the Willoughby police cars sitting just a hundred feet away with its blue lights flashing. Officer Clark had brought it down while the digging progressed. I've never liked Officer Clark, but at that moment, I could have hugged him.

Mr. Diamond knelt and scooped Lisa up in his arms. Officer Clark walked alongside holding the oxygen bottle while her father carried her to the car. "Put her in the back seat, Larry," Chief Ramsey instructed, opening the door for them. But at that moment we heard the wail of a siren and looked up to see an ambulance speeding down the gravel road, red lights flashing. They loaded Lisa onto a stretcher, and the ambulance took off in a spray of gravel.

Some of the crowd began to hike back to their cars, while others stayed behind to examine the crate where Lisa had been imprisoned. I stumbled along with the first group, hardly able to see the ground for the tears in my eyes. Had we found Lisa in time?

I felt a strong hand on my shoulder and looked up into the kind, strong face of Officer Bill. "Oh, Officer Bill," I cried, throwing my arms around him, "will Lisa be all right?"

He returned my hug. "I believe she'll live," he answered slowly, as though searching for words. "But there's always the possibility of brain damage. Apparently, she was without sufficient oxygen for a while because of the collapsed hose. And she went two days without insulin."

Sherlock joined us just then. "Pray for her, Penny," he said huskily. "Pray for her." He glanced away, but not before I saw the tears in his eyes.

The drive back to Willoughby seemed to take forever. Sherlock and I sat in the back of the FBI car, but no one said a word. We were all relieved that we had found Lisa, but we were also worried that we might have been too late. Agent Lewis dropped Sherlock and me off at our homes.

As I ate supper with my family, I told Mom and Dad all about the search for Lisa at the abandoned gypsum mine. When I came to the part about the rattlesnake, Mom turned pale. "You could have been killed," she whispered. She paused. "But I'm glad you went and helped."

The walkie-talkie began to beep right after supper, and I dashed upstairs to answer it. "Penny here. Over."

"I just got a call from Mr. Diamond," Sherlock told me. "Lisa's in General Hospital, and she's doing fine. She's conscious, and her heart rate and respiration have returned to nearly normal. I thought you'd want to know. Over."

"Thanks," I replied. "Is she going to be OK? Will there be any brain damage? Over."

"I guess it's too early to tell," Sherlock replied. "But Mr. Diamond seemed pleased with her progress. He and Mrs. Diamond are both at the hospital right now. Well, see you at church tomorrow. Over and out."

"Thanks for letting me know, Sherlock. By the way, you were fantastic! Over and out."

I slept very well that night.

The next morning during church Pastor Rogers told the congregation about the kidnapping. He called some of the deacons up front and had a special time of prayer for Lisa asking God for her full recovery. I prayed for her all during the sermon.

As Sherlock and I walked out of church with our parents, I was surprised to see Mr. Diamond out front, standing beside the limousine. He hurried up to us as we came out.

"I'm on my way to see Lisa," he said, "and I thought you might want to come along. Lisa has been asking about you."

"How is she?" I inquired. "Is she going to be OK?"

"You'll just have to wait and see for yourself," he told me, but the huge grin on his face told me what I needed to know.

He turned to our folks. "May Penny and Sherlock go with me? We can get lunch at the hospital."

We followed Mr. Diamond to the limousine, and he opened a rear door for us. The big car had two seats in the rear, facing each other, with a small table in between. There was even a small refrigerator under the table! I stepped in and was surprised to see Brandon Marshall.

"I . . . I asked if I could see Lisa too," he told us hesitantly.

I enjoyed the ride to Spencerville. The big car seemed to float along, and you didn't even feel the bumps in the road. Soft music and a soft drink from the refrigerator added to the luxury of the ride. But what I enjoyed most was the knowledge that Lisa was going to be all right.

Mr. Underwood dropped us off right in front of the hospital, and we followed Mr. Diamond inside. I could hardly wait to see Lisa. We took the elevator to the third floor, then stopped at Room 319 and pushed open the door.

Lisa was sitting up in bed, and her eyes lit up when we entered the room. "Come in, come in," she urged. "It's good to see you!" I was delighted to see that the color was back in her cheeks and the familiar cheerful sparkle was in her eyes. She was still the same Lisa.

I ran to the bed and leaned over to hug her, bumping against her IV tube as I did. "I'm sorry!" I blurted, feeling so clumsy. "I hope I didn't hurt you."

"Not at all," she said with a cheerful laugh. "They're gonna take this thing out tonight anyway. And I may get to go home tomorrow!"

Mrs. Diamond had been sitting on a small sofa in the corner of the room. She stood up and approached Lisa's bedside, smiling happily. "The doctor says that Lisa's doing just fine," she declared. "And believe me, we're thankful!"

Mr. Diamond turned to Sherlock. "My daughter owes her life to you, young man. We're very grateful."

My friend looked at the floor in embarrassment. "It was the Lord," he said modestly. "He showed us where to find her."

"Yes, but the Lord used you," the millionaire replied. "He used your intelligence and gift for noticing details to save her life. We give God the glory for Lisa's safe return, but we're also thanking you."

He pulled a check from his pocket. "Here's the reward I offered you the other day," he said, handing it to Sherlock. "I'm afraid that I must insist that you take it. Spend it, put it away for college, or do whatever you want with it. If your father has any questions, have him call me. But the money is yours to keep."

Sherlock looked at me. "Penny deserves half of it," he declared. "I'll split it with her." (And in the end, that's what he did. We each tithed on the money and then put the rest away for college.)

"And there's one more thing," the millionaire said, picking up a flat package wrapped in fancy gold paper. He handed it to Sherlock. "Penny said you'd like this."

Sherlock tore the paper from the package to find a huge butterfly mounted on blue velvet inside a Plexiglas display case. "A Queen Alexandra's Birdwing!" he said excitedly.

Mr. Diamond nodded, pleased at Sherlock's reaction. "Do you know how hard it is to locate one of those things? We thought we'd never find one!"

Sherlock grinned, still examining the butterfly with delight. "It's a perfect specimen, sir. Thank you!"

Brandon approached Lisa hesitantly. He pulled a wrinkled tract from his shirt pocket and handed it to her. "Thanks for giving me this," he said shyly. "I guess I read it a million times."

He glanced at us, then back to Lisa. "I wanted you to know that I did what it said," he informed her softly. "I asked Jesus to save me from my sins."

Lisa smiled that beautiful smile of hers. "I'm very glad, Brandon. I'm very, very glad."

I was delighted to notice that the diamond heart bracelet was back on her wrist. "I have a confession to make," I told her quietly. "Before I met you, I had already decided that you were going to be a real snob, and I made up my mind not to like you. But you're already one of my best friends! I guess I learned how foolish it is to judge people before you get to know them."

Lisa started to respond, but I held up one hand to stop her. "And there's something else," I continued. "I envied you because you were so rich. Sherlock kept telling me that money doesn't make people happy, but I refused to believe him. I do now! In a way, it was your family's money that caused this whole kidnapping. So I guess I'm glad I'm not rich. I'm asking God to teach me to be content with whatever He gives me."

Lisa looked thoughtful. "I have to admit that I did some thinking in the last couple of days too," she replied. "I've never thought it was all that special to be rich. In fact, sometimes I hate it because people treat me so differently. But I realized yesterday that I've been trusting in our family's money instead of in the Lord. Every time we had any kind of a problem, Daddy's money would take care of it. This was one time that money couldn't help, and I had to depend on the Lord."

Mrs. Diamond wiped tears from her eyes. "You aren't the only one who learned that yesterday," she replied.

Mr. Diamond moved closer. "Well, we had better say goodbye and let Lisa get some rest. Let's run down to the cafeteria and find some of that good hospital food, shall we?"

He leaned over and kissed Lisa, and then the rest of us said our goodbyes. We started out of the room, but Lisa called me back. "Penny."

I turned around. "Yes, Lisa?"

"Be sure to get my books tomorrow after school, and copy the homework assignments down for me, will you? I'll be back at school Tuesday."

I laughed as I left the room. "I'll be glad to, Lisa," I called back. "There's nothing I'd like better!"